TOKYO

ALL ALONE IN THE BIG CITY

GRAHAM MARKS

First published in Great Britain in 2006 by Bloomsbury Publishing Plc
36 Soho Square, London, W1D 3QY

Copyright © Graham Marks 2006
The moral right of the author has been asserted

A CIP catalogue record of this book is available from the British Library

ISBN 0 7475 8172 X
ISBN 9780747581727

All papers used by Bloomsbury Publishing are natural, recyclable products made
from wood grown in well-managed forests. The manufacturing processes conform
to the environmental regulations of the country of origin.

Typeset by Dorchester Typesetting Group Ltd
Printed in Great Britain by Clays Ltd, St Ives Plc

1 3 5 7 9 10 8 6 4 2

www.bloomsbury.com
www.marksworks.co.uk

This book is dedicated
to the memory of Keith Miller
1947–2005
Take the very best care of your friendships

Author's note:

All the chapter titles are genuine examples of straight-up Enganese (or Janglish) which I found in Tokyo. They don't make any sense in Japan either, and aren't meant to be relevant to the chapters. They're just a part of the journey. Make your own sense of them.

1

Dream for you

A phone had started ringing in Adam's dream. An insistent, annoying, faraway noise that made his dream-self tense and aggravated, edgy because there was something he knew he should be doing but couldn't. The sound was out of place, worrying, in a low-grade kind of way . . . and then he woke up, dragged out of his stupor by the silence which followed the phone in his parents' room being picked up. Night-time hearing, which seemed to amplify every tiny noise, picked up muffled voices, and under his door he saw lights being turned on. Adam peered at his alarm clock, saw it was approaching 2:00 a.m., and sat up. There was no such thing as a good-news phone call at this time of night.

He figured it must have been something to do with his Grannie Angie, his mum's mum, who was losing it big time, like old people do when bits, fairly important bits that we all take pretty much for granted, start going wrong. She was on the way out and he knew she was going to peg it, and probably sooner rather than later. The other worry was what would happen to Granpa Eddy when she did eventually go. Adam had heard his parents discussing that he couldn't look after himself, that there was no way he'd go into a home, but where would he live?

Lying back down in bed, eyes closed, he'd hoped, in the way that people prayed cos they believed it really made a difference, that Grangie, like they'd always called her, was all right. That nothing bad had happened, at least not yet. He knew it would eventually, bound to, but please, please, please, not right now.

Later Adam realised he must've fallen back to sleep, the way you can do sometimes, like a switch being turned off, because the next thing he knew his room was ablaze with harsh electric light and he could hear his name being growled.

Forcing his eyes open he saw his dad was standing at the door. He looked grey and dishevelled, his hair sticking out at odd angles and his chin dark with stubble. It was something about his father's expression that really woke Adam up, a steely anger in his eyes that he'd only ever seen once before, that time, back in Year 11, when he'd been caught truanting.

Adam scratched his head, yawning. 'What's up, Dad?'

'How long have you known, Adam?'

'Known what?'

'That Charlie was working in some bar in Tokyo.'

Ah, that . . .

Charlie. The house seemed so empty – even with three people and a dog rattling round in it – since she'd gone. Adam's sister, twenty-one, only three years older than him, but one of those annoyingly bright people who breeze through school and uni, hardly seeming to break into a sweat, had been away since early January. She was now nearly five months into her round-the-world-trip-of-alifetime, and Adam missed her.

There were a lot of things he didn't miss, like the needling comments his parents made about why couldn't he be more like her academically, and the way she borrowed whatever she wanted – clothes, CDs, Walkman – without asking. But life without Charlie around was, well, dull. It hadn't always been like that. They'd hated each other for years, fighting like mortal enemies until, quite suddenly, around the time his face had stopped erupting like Mount Vesuvius, peace had broken out instead and they'd become best friends. Weird, but there you go.

Plus, with his sister not around, Adam was now the sole focus of his parents' attention, the target for all their angst, the next project to be completed. He felt like a lab rat, part of an experiment to see if it was possible to create failure out of a passion for success – could you make someone bomb their A levels by caring way too much about them passing? He wanted to sit them down and explain what they were doing to him, but he knew they'd never listen. Charlie usually acted as his Defence Minister, able to intervene when things got bad, deflecting sniper fire and opening conciliation talks, but she wasn't here.

And now the heavy artillery was going off big time.

2

Be genteel

Thing was, Charlie wasn't supposed to be in Japan. The last postcard she'd sent had been from Vietnam, from where she and Alice – best friend from school, also doing the year-off travel thing, usual story – were planning on going to China and from there make their way down to Australia and then New Zealand. That had been maybe two months ago, but Charlie was crap at keeping in touch and no one had been at all surprised by the lack of post or email. Except Adam had been getting emails. But he hadn't said anything because he'd been sworn to secrecy about the girls' change of plans.

When you're travelling, Adam knew, things get fluid, circumstances can dictate a move other than had previously been on the cards. You could meet someone you like who's going somewhere else; you could lose all your money and have to re-route to where you can earn some quick bucks; maybe you simply get bored and fancy going to a different place. Charlie and Alice had ended up in Tokyo through a combination of all these events.

It was Alice, Adam remembered, who met someone in Hanoi – Steve, from Brighton . . . all that way to hook up with some bloke from Brighton – and it was in Shanghai where the plans had gone tits up when Charlie had all her money stolen, although Alice was pretty broke by then too. Steve-from-Brighton was the one who'd come up with the bright idea of going to Japan. According to Charlie, he'd been to Australia and was really up for Tokyo; Alice, who was apparently stuck to the guy like gaffer tape, thought Tokyo sounded *brilliant*, especially as this Steve person maintained it'd be dead easy for the girls to earn enough cash there for the rest of the trip. Businessmen just loved to sit in bars and talk to pretty English hostesses, he'd said. Yeah, right.

Adam hadn't liked the sound of Steve, or his ideas for how Alice and Charlie could get some more cash. Which was exactly how Charlie knew their parents would feel, but times it by a hundred, so she'd made Adam swear not to say anything. She wasn't so keen on the idea either, but she didn't want to carry on travelling by herself and she wasn't ready to come home; they'd get the money, move on and no one would be any the wiser. Yeah, right.

Adam felt totally spaced. It was now something like 2:35 a.m., as stated by the digital display on the oven, he was downstairs in the kitchen being given the third degree by his parents and he hadn't even been allowed to get himself a drink or anything. It also didn't help that he hadn't quite got his head round the fact that Charlie had disappeared.

'What did Alice actually say, Mum?'

'I told you.' His mother, sitting opposite Adam at the table, looked older yet somehow frail and childlike at the same time; she turned away and Adam saw a tear run down her face. In the corner of the room, sitting and watching,

Badger, their black and white mongrel, got out of his basket and walked over to sit next to her.

'She said that she hasn't seen Charlie since Saturday night.' Adam's dad, circling the perimeter of the kitchen like a nervous guard, stopped and stared at him. 'She was hysterical, hard to make sense of, but the gist of it was that the last time she'd seen Charlie she was going off with some Japanese businessman – how long have you known she was working as a . . . as a bloody bar girl, Adam?'

Adam saw his mother look at him, waiting to hear what he said, the expression on her face making him feel like whatever had happened was all his fault.

'Look, Mum, she asked me not to say anything, cos you'd just get worried.'

'Why were they doing it?'

'They needed the money. Charlie'd had most of hers stolen in Shanghai, but she didn't want to come home yet so they went to Tokyo. Her and Alice and Alice's boyfriend.'

'Why didn't she just ask us to send some money out to her?' Adam's dad began pacing again. 'She could've paid us back later, she didn't have to go *prostituting* herself, for God's sake!'

'Tony!' Shocked, Adam's mum wiped tears from her cheek with the back of her hand. 'I'm sure she wasn't . . .'

'She was only doing hostess work, Dad . . . she just wanted to do this trip by herself, asking you for money would've been, I dunno, cheating. She said she wanted to do it her way.'

'And look where it bloody got her!'

'Dad, we don't know . . .'

'Exactly, Adam, exactly – we don't *know* anything, we can't *do* anything . . .'

'Dad, I'm sorry . . .' Adam glanced across the table at his mum, who seemed to be frozen in a state of panic. 'Have you called the police? At least we can do that.'

3

Keep off the pond

Adam was knackered. Since just after three he'd been unable to sleep; they'd all gone back to bed after his dad had first called the police, but all he'd done was wait for them to arrive. By the looks of his parents, that's exactly what they'd done as well. And even though he had the perfect excuse not to go into college today, the thought of hanging round the house, trying to dodge the cloud of blame that was following him around, was too much.

The police were now downstairs in the lounge with his parents,.presumably going over the details of what Alice had said when she'd called. They'd arrived almost an hour ago, but, as Adam hadn't actually heard what she'd said, there was little else he could do once he'd handed over a print-out of Charlie's last email, so he'd disappeared back up to his room, followed by Badger.

Adam showered, first cold then hot, to help clear his fuzzed-up head, got dressed, and went down to the kitchen, where he made himself a very strong cup of black coffee to kick his brain into action. As he drank it he kind of wished he hadn't given up smoking, but he had, cos Suzy, his still-quite-new girlfriend, had made it a compulsory proviso to him going out with her. Right now, though, lighting one up would, along with the coffee and sugar hit, be the booster rocket that'd get him out of the gravity pull of the house; it was the perfect morning chemistry equation – caffeine, plus glucose, with an added dash of nicotine to balance everything out.

As he was about to make good his escape, one of the two plain-clothes officers who'd come to the house snared him by the front door. He looked like any of the policemen you see on the TV news, giving interviews to a forest of microphones: a vaguely nondescript bloke in a dark grey suit, a scattering of dandruff on his shoulders, smelling of aftershave and tobacco and with a slightly quizzical expression.

'Going?'

'Yeah,' Adam looked down at his watch. 'Late for college . . .'

'So you knew your sister was in Tokyo, working at that bar, the one she mentioned in her email?' Adam nodded, looking back at the kitchen door where Badger now sat, watching. 'And you didn't say anything?' The officer let the question hang, accusingly, in the air.

'I already explained to the other guy, she asked me not to.' Adam turned and held the man's gaze. 'It wasn't a big deal.'

'Well, it is now, sunshine, and from now on, you let us know the moment you hear anything from anyone. OK?'

'You think I'm hiding something?'

'You have, you might again.' The officer shrugged, smiling, and moved out of Adam's way so he could get to the front door. 'Just wanted to make sure you understood that the rules have changed.'

'Rules?'

'Until we can ascertain what's happened to Charlotte, this

is a police investigation and withholding information is against the rules.'

Adam felt himself redden. 'Why would I withhold information? You think I don't want Charlie to be found?'

The police officer looked over his shoulder, back at the lounge where his colleague was still talking to Adam's parents. He lowered his voice.

'At the moment I don't know what to think. I'm just asking, politely, that you don't do anything out of a misplaced sense of loyalty to your sister that would hinder us in doing our job. That's all.'

Normally Adam would have waited at the stop for a bus, but he felt like he needed a walk to sort out some of the shit that was cluttering up his head. In such a short time – it was only eight hours or so since Alice had called – his whole world seemed to have been picked up, shaken and spun round till he didn't know which way was up.

Charlie was missing, she was somewhere, thousands of miles away, and they had no idea where or with whom. And the police were involved, covering everything you thought or did with an aura of suspicion, as if guilt was something you carried with you like a disease. Thing was, he did feel guilty for not telling his parents about Charlie and Alice's change of plans, even though logic dictated that it probably wouldn't have changed anything. Still . . .

Walking past a small newsagent's, Adam almost veered left and went in. A siren whisper in his head was saying, 'Just one cigarette . . .', but he knew if he turned up at college smelling of fags, Suzy would go ape-shit and that would simply add to his already dismal mood. Right now he needed TLC, not telling off.

4

Parody market

Adam woke up the next morning, slowly coming to with a song playing in his head. This wasn't unusual, he quite often had a soundtrack to accompany the start of his day, but this song was different. It was a blues song which he'd originally heard as a sample on a tune by some hip-hop artist. Only available as a white label, no details, it'd taken him weeks to track down who had done the original version. Finally he'd discovered it was called 'Everyday I Have the Blues', sung by a bloke called Lowell Fulson.

This wasn't something you could just walk into Woolworth's and find on the shelf with the Top 40 and the repackaged collections of 60s, 70s and 80s stuff – all that any high-street shop seemed to carry nowadays. It did make you wonder when the charity shops had the most interesting selection of vinyl, tapes and CDs. He'd eventually found the track, through a site on the web, on a CD called *Juke Box Shuffle*.

Adam got up, wandered over to his veteran, sticker-covered mini-system, flicked through a pile of CDs until he found what he wanted – Lowell smiling at him on the cover, all cool dude, pencil moustache, smoking a cigarette – and put it on. The sound of a piano picking out a jazzy, 12-bar blues filled the room, followed by the drummer's brushes, a soulful clarinet and then the voice, singing about loss and how bad it felt. How terminally shitty it was to be alone.

It was simple, no technology, no studio tricks. Music and nothing else. He imagined a group of friends, sitting on old wooden chairs in some bar room, just jamming together, making music because that's how they dealt with life. As he listened to the song Adam could see it all in his mind's eye; in the corner of a room, the bluesmen were sitting playing in shafts of sunlight, motes of dust falling upwards, driven by the heat of the day.

As the final note was blown and the voice died away, Adam came back to his room, his reality, his own personal loneliness. He quickly switched CDs and put on the last Foo Fighters album. Loud, driven, mindless, with a beat like a heart about to explode. You couldn't feel sad listening to it, you just felt numbed by the sonic punch. Aural painkiller.

'Adam!'

He turned and saw Suzy waving at him from across the road as he got off the bus. He waved back, feeling better the moment he saw her. Suzy'd never met Charlie, as she was already off on her travels when they became an item, but yesterday, as Adam had told her everything that had happened, she'd listened and at the end convinced him it wasn't in any way his fault, that it would all be OK. She'd managed his panic and calmed him down.

'Adam, have you seen the paper?' Suzy was waving one of the tabloids at him as he crossed the road.

'No, what about it?'

'They've got the story.'

'Story?'

'About Charlie, there's a thing about Charlie going missing . . .'

Adam grabbed the paper. 'Where?'

'A couple of pages in . . . on a right-hand page.'

'How could they know . . . ?' Adam hurriedly scanned the pages as he turned them, and then he saw the headline: BRIT BAR GIRL MISSING. It was a small news piece, only a couple of very short columns and no picture; Adam stood and read it quickly, then read it again, not quite believing what he was seeing on the page.

> In an eerie echo of what happened to Lucie Blackman in 2000, another Brit bar girl, Charlotte Grey, 25, has gone missing from a club in the Roppongi district of Tokyo where she worked as a hostess earning £100 an hour. Last seen in the company of an unidentified Japanese man on Saturday night, Charlotte, who is on a gap-year trip, was reported missing by her travelling companion after she failed to return to the flat they were sharing. Like Lucie Blackman, who was murdered by businessman Joji Obara, 48, Charlotte did not have a visa and was working illegally. Police are investigating.

'How on earth could they have got to know so quickly, Adam?'

'No idea, but it's a load of crap . . .' Adam closed the newspaper and gave it back to Suzy. 'All they got right was the fact she's missing. Her age is wrong, she's not on a gap year and there's no way she was earning £100 an hour, that's just crap. Makes her sound like a complete tart, too, and they're assuming she's been murdered like that other girl. God, I hope my parents don't see the story – how did you know about it? You never buy a paper.'

'Andy showed it me, on the bus.'

'Shit, that means the whole bloody school'll know in two seconds flat.'

'I asked him to keep quiet . . . he might.'

'Jeez . . .' It had to be Andy. Nice guy, best mate and everything, but a mouth that flapped like a duck landing on a pond. There was no way he'd keep this quiet. Adam felt like turning round and going straight home.

'Come on, we'll be late.' Suzy tugged his arm and nodded towards the school entrance.

They hadn't got more than fifty metres into the grounds when Adam heard his name being called and saw Steve Apperly, the kind of ego-heavy smartarse every year seemed to have to have at least one of.

Steve-bloody-Apperly.

Now Adam knew why he'd had a negative reaction to the news that Alice's boyfriend was called Steve. This one was with a couple of his mates and they had a paper which they were making a big thing of reading. Adam felt his stomach knot. It had started already.

'Hey, Adam, your sister must be quite something, right?' Steve Apperly was pointing at the page he and his mates were reading. 'What the hell does £100 an hour get you, fercrissake!'

'Some froth on your coffee!' One of the other boys smirked and dug his elbow into Steve's ribs.

Adam felt Suzy's grip tighten on his arm. 'Ignore them,' she whispered.

'Yeah, OK, but who's gonna tell them to ignore me, Suze?' Adam walked on. This, he knew, could only get worse.

5

Food/Drugs/Fish/School/Etc.

Whichever way he looked at it, this had been the week from hell. At home, with every day that there was no more news from Alice in Tokyo, and precious little in the way of progress from the police, Adam watched his mum approaching catatonic basket-case status. All she did was sit quietly by the phone and stare into the middle distance. He knew she was desperate, believing that a call was as likely to bring bad news as it was worse. As likely to tell her she'd lost a parent or a child.

His dad, on the other hand, was in a permanent mood of angry impotence, verbally lashing out at him and the dog out of frustration that there was nothing he could do. That, anyway, was what it felt like to Adam, who had other problems to deal with.

News about Charlie's disappearance had gone round college like a cold sore at a party, fuelled by an additional follow-up story in the papers on Thursday. It was basically just a re-hash of the earlier piece, along the lines of 'Girl still missing', only this time they'd somehow managed to get hold of a picture of Charlie. And Adam had a fair idea where they'd got it from. Steve Apperly's older sister and Charlie had been in the same year and tutor group, added to which Steve was all of a sudden striding around in a brand-new pair of very top-of-the-line Nikes. Do the math, as Adam's American cousin would've said.

For the most part the kidding had been good natured, if fairly constant and pretty low-rent. It wasn't hard to deal with, Adam found, if you just zoned it out. But Steve Apperly and friends were a different case altogether.

They were in his face all the time. They never gave up. They never got bored. It was as if they'd made it a personal mission to use their less than barbed wit to goad him at every possible opportunity, just to see how long it would take to break him.

In the end it took four days.

Coming out of a double English tutorial – almost two solid hours of Chaucer – Adam hadn't really been paying attention and had walked straight into the middle of Apperly and Crew. If he'd had his head in a different place he'd have spotted them and detoured, but as it was, there he was, surrounded.

'Look who's here . . .'

Adam glanced over at Steve, leaning up against a wall with a folded-up newspaper under one arm and smiling at him. 'Yeah, what a big surprise, eh, Steve? Me, here. Who'd have thought?'

Steve pushed himself off the wall and opened the paper. 'I see Charlie's in the news again. Nice picture.'

Someone behind Adam laughed.

Adam looked pointedly at Steve's feet.

'I see you got a new pair of trainers, Steve. Did your slag of a sister buy them for her little bruv?'

'Watch it, Grey, you leave my sister out of this.' Steve's

ears went bright red and his whole face pinched. 'She's not the one giving it up for £100 an hour in some sleazoid bar in Japan, man.'

'Right, I heard *she* did it for a lot less down the bogs at the Royal Oak.' Adam looked right at one of the guys with Steve, the short one with bad acne who he figured was least sure of himself, and nodded at him. 'You been there, Terry? I heard she does anyone, even guys with a rabid skin condition.'

Adam knew he was skating on no ice at all, antagonising both Steve and his spotty mate, but he had had it with backing off and soaking up the verbal sucker punches. This was payback time and it felt great to be giving as good as he'd been getting all week.

'I told you!' Steve yelled, leaning forward and shaking a vicious finger at Adam.

Adam grabbed it and bent it back further than it had ever been designed to go. 'And I wasn't listening . . .' Adam watched Steve gasp with pain, 'but you better had, Apperly. If you don't cut out all this crap I'm gonna –'

But Steve never found out what Adam was going to do because Terry waded in, yelling 'Bastard!', and threw a wild punch that made Adam's hand, still holding Steve's finger, jerk forward. Steve's scream, as his finger broke, was the signal for general mayhem to break out.

Adam found himself at the centre of a storm of wind-milling fists and pummelling feet, with at least one person – he soon realised it was Terry because he was yelling 'Bastard!' – clinging to his back; it felt like he was trying to bite his head. Running backwards and slamming into the wall got rid of the manic, bloodthirsty limpet for the moment, but there were still three more attackers ready, willing and able to finish him off.

They circled him, warily at first — Steve and Terry, proof Adam was no pushover, were still lying on the floor — and then they started to move in on him. Word of the fight had obviously got out because, as he whirled round trying to fend off blows, Adam realised there was now a sizeable audience shouting and cheering and all but drowning out Steve Apperly's keening wail as he lay on the floor, clutching his hand.

Adam knew there was no way he could win this fight, that he was, no doubt about it, going to come out way the worst off, but something drove him on. For every punch and kick he took he lashed out with more fury, an insistent, driven voice in his head repeating, mantra-like, 'How dare they take the piss out of Charlie, how dare they . . .' Then, as he felt his adrenaline-boosted strength draining away, through a pink mist he saw figures push their way through the baying crowd — more of Steve's friends come to have a go? — and, realising he had nothing left, he fell to his knees, head hanging down.

They hadn't been more attackers, but a couple of Deputy Heads and one of the Games Masters. The three boys who'd been fighting Adam had been sent to wait outside their Head of Year's office; Steve and Terry, who'd been knocked semi-conscious when he was smashed against the wall, were shipped off to the local hospital in an ambulance and Adam had been taken to the medical room to be checked over by the nurse.

'Blood, sweat and tears,' she said, cleaning up Adam's face with a stinging medicated swab to see if there was anything worse than superficial cuts and bruises to be dealt with.

'Not me crying, nurse.'

'Nothing to be proud of, sending two people to hospital.'

'I didn't throw the first punch.'

'Save your excuses for the powers that be, Adam,' said the nurse, throwing the bloodied swab into a bin. 'Now take off your shirt and let me check the rest of you – anything in particular hurt?'

'Just everything.'

'Anything like a sharp pain anywhere?' The nurse pressed the left side of Adam's bruised and grazed rib cage and watched for his reaction: nothing spectacular. 'You certainly took a beating. What was this all about?'

'Nothing.' Adam stared at the fish tank over by the wall, its tiny, brightly coloured inhabitants gliding through the fake coral reef environment, looking for a way out.

'Don't treat me like an idiot. This was about something, Adam . . . was it girl trouble?'

Adam winced as the nurse pushed in on his right side. 'Yeah, kind of . . .'

'You boys, testosterone has an awful lot to answer for.' The nurse handed Adam a glass of water. 'Rinse your mouth out and let me check your teeth.'

'They were dissing my sister.'

'Sorry?'

'My sister, Charlie . . . she's gone missing. In Japan.' Adam took a mouthful of water, rinsed and spat it out into the sink. 'There's been a story in the papers and those guys've been going at me all week, calling her a tart and stuff, and all she was doing was working in a bar. She told me –'

'Open wide.' The nurse shone a small torch into Adam's mouth. 'How long has she been missing?'

'Almost a week now.'

'I didn't know, I'm sorry. I'm sure she'll be fine, Adam.' The nurse switched the torch off. 'You'd better see a dentist, just in case anything's come loose, otherwise I think you're fine, considering. Nothing broken. Let me just dress the cuts and then, I'm afraid, you have to go and see the Headmaster.'

'At least he can't make me feel any worse than I already do.'

'Haven't you ever heard the old adage "sticks and stones may break my bones, but words can never hurt me"?'

'Yeah, and "turn the other cheek", but I've been doing that all week and I'd just had enough.' Adam put his shirt back on and did it up. 'And like I said, I didn't start it . . .'

Point of view. Weird, thought Adam, how it changed from person to person, and with it, the way whatever had happened was perceived. What was actually considered to be the truth depended on the point of view of the person with the final say. Which was OK if it was the same one as yours, but that was not always the case. The truth was, 'truth' turned out to be a fluid thing. Malleable, like putty, it could be bent to suit whoever held sway, whoever had the biggest stick.

If this was the way it happened in his headmaster's office, thought Adam, then why not anywhere, *everywhere* else? Who could you believe, who could be trusted to tell the truth? And was there ever an *absolute* truth? From his point of view, no.

'Like I said, sir, I didn't start it.' Adam was tired and beginning to think he must sound like a stuck CD. Even he was starting to find himself as unconvincing as the Headmaster obviously did.

'You may well think that, but two boys are in hospital

because of your actions and I am going to have to suspend you until all this is properly sorted out.' Mr Taylor rearranged some papers and a couple of pencils in front of him, then looked back up at Adam. 'I am really very sorry to hear about Charlotte, but, however badly you feel about her going missing, your behaviour was unacceptable. You will have to stay at home for at least the next week, maybe longer, and I will be in touch with your parents.'

And that was that.

6

Make you white

Adam had considered leaving it till Sunday evening to tell his parents about the suspension – less time for accusations, aggravation and shit dumping. He also felt bad that what he'd done would only add to the crap his mum and dad were having to deal with. Suzy, who'd been waiting for him when he came out of Mr Taylor's office, pointed out that a face covered in bruises and plasters was a bit of an advert for something being up and that he probably didn't have the option of waiting.

Put that way Adam had to agree, and went straight home to face the music, which turned out not to be as bad as he'd imagined it might. Strange, he thought, how you never seemed to be able to second-guess how parents were going to react to what you'd done. Often they blew their collective stack over the most trivial thing, going totally ballistic about some microscopic event – which, apparently, you'd been told about a *million* and one times before – and then they could act so calm about something heinous you'd done, it was hard not to believe they'd gone temporarily deaf and hadn't heard what you'd told them.

His dad's reaction to the events at school – a raised eyebrow, a small, wry smile, a pat on the back and the reassurance that everything would be sorted out – led Adam to believe he'd felt like punching someone out, too. That, like Adam, his dad somehow felt better for the action Adam'd taken, even if it had achieved nothing positive. He hadn't shouted at him, or anything.

Adam's mum had cried again, but then got very busy, insisting on changing all the plasters, saying that she'd ring the dentist first thing in the morning and also make an appointment for him to be checked out by the family's GP. He started trying to tell her he was all right, but it dawned on him that this was the first time in a week he'd seen his mum so energised. She had something to do, someone to look after; someone right there she could actually take care of. So he let her.

Up in his room, Badger curled in a ball under his desk, farting silently, Adam logged on and checked his email. Nothing new from Charlie. But, because it was still there, he opened up the last message he'd had from her and stared at it.

> *Tokyos amazing, Ad!!!!!! Alice, Steve and me have this t-i-n-y place (still costs a bloody fortune) and were working in a place called the Bar Belle, Ali and me anyway. Steves got a gig at a kebab stand (yes, tyhey have doner kebabs here!!!!). Were on the late shift, but thats when the tips are best – the punters are so pissed they dont know what theyre giving you a lot of the tiem!!! This areas called High Touch Town, but dont get the wrong idea all we do is serve drinks and talk to customers, blokes in suits (they all look the same Ad,*

honest to god) who just seem to think its SO COOL to sit and chitchat with us!!! Got to go, and remember, for godssake don't breathe a word to M+D! Chasxxxxxx

Re-reading it – classic Charlie style, full of spelling mistakes and exclamation marks, empty of punctuation – he could hear her voice, feel her enthusiasm, touch her spirit. With Charlie everything had to be fast – like even though Charlie was short for Charlotte it wasn't short enough, and she always signed herself 'Chas'. Adam couldn't imagine that this message, these few words up on his computer screen, would be the last he'd ever hear from her.

How could she be missing? Maybe she and Alice had had an argument and she'd just gone off to stay with some new friend for a bit. Maybe she didn't like Steve, didn't like being the gooseberry in that relationship and had moved out without telling anyone. Charlie could be a bit impulsive sometimes. Except she would have told him. They always told each other their troubles, their news, and while she was crap at sending postcards, Charlie would – when she remembered – send him some kind of message via email, even if it was like the one from Vietnam that had just said *'hi. hanoi. hot hot hot. c x'.*

And it was now ten days since her last contact. There was no way this was good. Something was wrong, something had *gone* wrong, and Charlie obviously needed help. But what was happening? Sweet FA.

Adam felt tired, but not go-to-bed tired. He was also far too jumpy – like he'd drunk more coffee than was good for him – to attempt vegging out in front of the TV, so he surprised the hell out of Badger by hauling him downstairs and taking him out for a very late walk round the block. It was a clear night, cool but not cold, and Adam wondered what it was like, halfway across the world in Tokyo.

He didn't actually know exactly how far away Japan was, or what the time difference was, geography not being something he'd ever been interested in. There had to be an atlas somewhere back at the house, and he made a mental note to find it when he got home. Charlie was out there – he had to believe still alive – in a strange foreign city; she was either being Charlie and just forgetting to keep in touch, or in such deep trouble she *couldn't* keep in touch.

In front of him, Adam watched Badger doing the dog thing. Not a care in the world, fed, watered and able to take a piss whenever and wherever you chose. Lucky bastard. Badger stopped and looked back at him, tongue out and tail lazily wagging, the expression on his face saying, 'Yeah, I don't give too much of a shit about anything, me . . .'

Reaching up to touch the collage of plasters, swellings and bruises on his face, Adam knew what it felt like to care too much. Although he hadn't been the one to throw the first punch, he knew he could've simply walked away and not got himself all riled and pumped up by that stupid shithead Apperly. The fight had been his fault, he'd made it happen, though there was no way he was ever going to admit that out loud and in public to anyone, even Suzy; and it hadn't solved anything. Right now, hours afterwards, even the sweet taste of victory – he had, after all, pulverised Steve and Terry – was turning sour.

When he got back, Adam thought about sending Charlie an email, but in the end decided not to. It would feel like uttering an electronic whisper, like calling out her name in some vast, empty house with thousands and thousands of rooms, on the off chance she was listening. Blatantly useless.

7

Beyond image

'God, man, you look gruesome . . .' Andy Cornwell stood staring at Adam in mock horror. 'Don't you think dark glasses, a hat and maybe a touch of cover-up might've been called for? You know, possibly a ski mask, seeing as you're out in public?'

'Leave it out, Andy.' Suzy appeared at the table with a couple of bottles of lager. 'Why don't you make yourself useful for once and get another round in before the bar gets overrun?'

'Since when did it become *my* round?'

'Since you went blabbing about Charlie all round the common room.' Adam smiled up at Andy as he pulled a chair out so Suzy could sit down.

'I swear to God,' Andy put both his hands up, 'I am innocent of the charges being made against me, man – Suzy asked me to zip the lip and I did, honest. Other people buy papers you know, and they don't *all* just look at page 3 and the sports reports. Even Steve Apperly, who we all know moves his lips when he reads.'

Adam grinned, then winced and rubbed his chin. 'Yeah well, get a round in anyway, would you?' He held up his bottle. 'Same again, mate – I'd go but my face hurts.'

Suzy, watching Andy walking away, got out her mobile and put it on the table. 'How do you feel?'

'Physically?' Suzy nodded as she took a drink. 'Like I've been used as a punchbag, but no surprises there, right?'

'And *in* your head, rather than *on* it?'

Adam nodded slowly, looking out of the pub window. 'I feel bloody useless, Suze, know what I mean? There's nothing I can do, except wait for something to happen . . . feels like, I don't know . . . I'm getting totally nowhere.' He looked back at Suzy, her short black hair shining in the sunlight like each strand had been individually polished, her big, dark brown eyes – each surrounded by thick, curved lashes, their lids glistening with a faint aura of pale gold – staring quizzically back at him. He held up his right hand. 'I feel like punching something, but I've already done that and it does not help, does not help at all. Got any bright ideas?'

Suzy shook her head. 'Nope.'

'Well, you're a big help.' Adam glanced over towards the pub's front door. 'Anyone else coming?'

'Ed and Mickey said they might pop in after their five-a-side match. Trisha and Sara and Pat've gone into town.'

'Just us and Andy then . . .' Adam was getting that a-fag-would-be-a-nice-idea feeling and wished he wasn't somewhere every other person seemed to be smoking. 'I nearly sent Charlie an email last night. I looked Tokyo up, it was seven in the morning on Saturday – today – cos they're eight hours ahead. It'd sort of be like time travel, really, sending a message to tomorrow . . .'

'You're rambling, Ad.'

'Kind of you to mention it, Suze . . . but if I talk I don't feel trapped in my head, which, as no one in my house is doing much in the way of conversation at the moment, happens a lot.'

'What does?' Andy appeared at the table holding four bottles and a couple of packets of crisps, and dumped them in the middle of the table before sitting down on the spare chair.

'Sitting round waiting for the phone to ring is driving me nuts, Andy, that's all.'

Right on cue Suzy's mobile began to ring; she grabbed it and Adam reached over to get a packet of crisps.

'I was just telling Suzy, Tokyo's eight hours ahead of us.'

'They're a light year ahead of us when it comes to gizmos.' Andy took a handful of crisps out of the open packet Adam was holding. 'I always flick through the gadget mags in the newsagent and check out what we're gonna be getting a year from now.'

Suzy put her phone back down on the table. 'That was Trisha . . . should she buy the red shoes or the pale blue ones. Like how would *I* know?'

'What did you say?' Adam offered her the crisps.

'I said see if they'd let her buy one of each.'

'Good thinking, Batwoman!' Andy leant across the table and clinked Suzy's bottle with his. 'Lateral. By the way, did you hear, that bloke Terry whatsisname and the other three who were with Steve Apperly have been suspended for ten days, like you, but Steve hasn't.'

Adam frowned. 'Why not?'

'Cos he wasn't actually involved in the fight, cos he was lying on the ground moaning the whole time, right? But he's taking the time off anyway as his right hand's all bandaged up and stuff and he can't write or use a keyboard or anything. Did it make a noise when it broke . . . you know, his finger?'

'I wasn't listening, Andy.' Adam made a 'you dolt' face. 'I was a bit preoccupied at the time, wasn't I.'

Andy put his empty bottle on the table. 'What're you gonna do with your holiday?'

'So not a holiday. There was a letter this morning, from Tyndal, saying he expected all my essays to be handed in when I come back Monday after next. I can think of better things to do.'

Suzy held up her phone. 'Which shoes should Trisha buy?'

Andy ignored Suzy. 'Like what?'

'Do *some*thing about Charlie . . . my parents just sit around waiting for the phone to ring and as far as I can see, the cops just sit around not phoning them. And my gran's not too chipper, either, so there aren't many laughs in my house right now, know what I mean?' Adam slumped in his chair and attempted to play a tune by blowing across the top of his half-empty bottle. 'And I get my head bitten off if I try and suggest anything . . . I just want to know what's happened to her, Andy, that's all.'

'Get on the next plane to Japan and show 'em how to do it, Sherlock!'

'I was thinking more along the lines of a sensible idea, Cornwell, something practical.'

'How about another round?'

8

My soul

It was two in the morning – 10:00 a.m. Tokyo time, as the small digital alarm clock he'd reset to be eight hours ahead reminded him. Adam was back home, alone. Suzy had wanted him to go back to hers, but he felt he couldn't risk not being around if – when – there was a phone call from Alice, the police, or even, hope of hopes, Charlie herself. Under the rules of the superstitious logic which now governed his life, being out in the day was OK, but it wasn't during the small hours.

So why hadn't he suggested Suzy come back to his place? Actually, why had she *never* been back to his place, never met his parents or anything? He'd spent plenty of time over at her house, in fact had left so many clothes there that Suzy's mum had even washed and dried them for him. Adam knew the answer, and it wasn't terribly complex or psychological, just that he felt so much under the microscope at home that he needed privacy. His own space. Which, under the circumstances – still being at sixth form college – was so not going to happen.

Suzy's place was the next best thing, a very acceptable substitute for somewhere of his own, because her parents expected nothing of him except reasonable manners, reasonable behaviour and no smoking within ten metres of the house. What did they care what his A Level passes were or which university he was going to go to and what he was going to do when he got his degree? They might be interested, but they didn't *care*. To them, Adam knew, he probably came across as a likeable, easygoing kind of guy; with them he was able to be. He liked who he was with them.

Now he thought about it, though, it was kind of odd that Suzy had never mentioned that she hadn't met his parents, had never asked to go round to his house. He'd never analysed it before, but theirs was a very cool relationship – as in 'not hot'. Like, they looked good together and got on really well, but it wasn't *spiced*, not a mad passion. Suzy was very practical and down-to-earth about things . . . like at the pub, just coming out and telling him he was rambling. Maybe, in her no-nonsense way, she simply didn't care whether she met his mum and dad or not.

His parents were sort of the same. They knew he had a new girlfriend, and his mum had recently made the occasional oblique reference to the fact that he was 'staying out with friends' a lot, but she wasn't that bothered. Them not having met Suzy was all part of the privacy thing – she had to be an enigma, exclusive, a secret. And in the end his parents were actually more interested in keeping up the pressure on him to get the results that would, to use their phrase, put him on the right road for a brilliant career. Right now, though, a brilliant career was the last thing on his mind. In fact, the more Adam thought about it, the less he felt like following the path he felt his parents had so carefully mapped out for him.

For a long time he'd never questioned his life. He worked hard, like he was expected to, and he played sports hard too; he always came pretty near the top and, when it happened, it felt good to win. But now, alone in his room, staring at Charlie's last email message, he didn't see the point any more.

Both his parents were smart people, his mum something high up in healthcare services and his father some big cheese statistics whiz in a market research company; not rich, but clever, because in their world it was brains not bucks that counted. Adam looked up at the poster on his wall, the one his mother hated, with the drooling cartoon dimwit saying *'We don' need no ejakayshun!'*. Rationally he knew he did need it, but what was the point of learning stuff if it didn't help you do things when things needed to get done? Like finding your missing sister.

Watching his parents helplessly waiting for events to unfold, rather than actively being involved in the process, kept reminding him that, in the real world, actions truly did speak louder than words.

Adam wanted to go and wake them up and tell them, remind them of this fact, but it was almost three now (nearly 10:56 a.m. in Tokyo . . .) and doing that would, he was sure, go down as well as a bag of cold sick. Tiredness settled over his shoulders like a dark, heavy blanket, making him sag, but he didn't want to go to bed having done nothing, although at this time of night, in this room, there was little he *could* do that would make any sort of difference. He looked over at the computer. Send an email out to Charlie? No point. She was missing, not sitting in some Internet café thinking about home. He glanced at the clock and wondered what it was like in Tokyo this morning.

Sitting down at the keyboard, he exited his email and logged on to the Net, Googling the word 'Tokyo' to see where he'd end up. He found the weather forecast for the next five days (a typhoon was due, then a couple of overcast days followed by temperatures and humidity beginning to rise to the low 30s); he read reviews for the top bars and clubs; he checked out a selection of 'mid-priced' hotels; he discovered that there were around 200 Yen to the pound, which meant, he worked out, that 'mid-priced' was not exactly cheap; and then he found a site that took him on a photographic tour of the city. It looked cool, with its mix of high-rise chrome, glass and garish fluorescent signs alongside elegant temples, exotic white-faced women dressed in kimonos and delicate, precise gardens.

Adam blinked, feeling like he'd fallen down, eyes wide open, in a sand pit, and he realised he'd been staring at the same image on the computer for so long that the screen saver had kicked in and he hadn't even noticed. Definitely time for bed. He logged off, shut down and crashed out.

9

We offer good sense and technique to you

Adam woke, rolling over to check the little alarm clock, and found the digital display read 20:05. Eight in the evening? Surely . . . then he remembered he'd set the clock to Tokyo time and checked his watch. Almost midday. Charlie had been missing for more than a week now. The realisation cleared the last of the sleep mists from his head and Adam sat up, rubbing the heels of his palms into his eyes and yawning so hard it felt as if someone was pulling his face apart.

Another day.

Well, half a day if you wanted to split hairs. And what was going to happen? More than likely sod all, just like the last six days. Sod all about Charlie, anyway. Every time it seemed like the moment had come when action would finally be taken, like *someone* would get on a bloody plane and go to Tokyo, something would happen to stop it. And the something was either Grangie getting worse, or Granpa Eddy falling apart because she was getting worse.

His mum was an only child – there was nobody else around to help take the strain, to help deal with the emotional nightmare of sick and ageing parents. He could see it was tearing his parents apart, not knowing what to do, and Adam could taste their frustration, like bile rising up in his throat; he felt bad that there were times he wished that his grandparents weren't there, that they would simply not exist, just for a week, so their daughter and son-in-law could move out of orbit and do something about Charlie.

God, he felt guilty when he thought things like that. Why wasn't there *something* he could do? Because staying in the bloody house for much longer was going to drive him certifiably nuts.

He sat on the edge of his bed, eyes flitting here and there, brain not really seeing what they were looking at. His gaze fell on his collection of all the different brands of bottled lager he'd ever drunk, up on the top shelf of his bookcase: there was Mexican, Chinese, German, Thai, Czech, American, Japanese, French. It was like a beer atlas, and looking at the bottles brought back what Andy had said to him in the pub: *'Get on the next plane to Japan and show 'em how to do it, Sherlock!'*

Adam stayed staring at the bottles, the words 'Why not?' being whispered in his ear by that guerrilla part of his mind he imagined had to be in charge of mad thoughts and idiot behaviour. But, then again, why the hell not? Clearly the real questions here were 'How?' and 'When?'. Trouble was, even though, since he was suspended, he had the time to do it, he didn't have the kind of cash that would allow him to waltz into a travel agent and buy himself a ticket to Tokyo. And his credit rating would not let him hit the plastic and worry about it later. 'What have I got in my pocket?' he heard the voice say, 'Not a lot . . .'

He wondered if this was how it was for schizophrenics all the time, constant two-way conversations in their head, back-and-forth arguments with their other selves. What was he supposed to do? Say to his dad that, as he wasn't getting off his arse to do anything, could he buy him a ticket so *he* could go and look for Charlie? Adam didn't think that was ever going to come true. In another, parallel universe maybe, but not on this timeline.

So how was it ever going to happen – was he going to have to rob a bank? Secretly borrow the money from the rich uncle he didn't have? Buy a lottery ticket or two and hope his number came up? There had to be a way, but Adam realised he was very hungry and needed to eat before he could think straight about anything, let alone the fantasy of how he'd get to Japan.

Adam sat back from the kitchen table and pushed his plate away from him. 'Fantastic fry-up, Mum. Just what I needed.'

'My pleasure.' His mum smiled, looking happier than he'd seen her in days. 'Remember to rinse your plate before you put it in the dishwasher, won't you.'

'You don't have to remind me *every* time.'

'And I don't tell you *every* time, just most of the time . . . and would you mind going through that pile of post over there?' His mother nodded at a small heap of letters stacked up on the work surface. 'I think it's mostly junk mail, but you never know, and it's recycling tomorrow.'

'OK.' Adam cleared up his dirty plate and cutlery and picked up the letters, flicking through them. His mum was right, mostly junk and at least four companies trying to get him to switch to their credit card. He started tearing up the envelopes, unopened. 'Don't you think it's bloody stupid the way –' He stopped, mid-sentence.

'The way what?'

'Oh, nothing . . .' Adam had remembered, as he was ripping stuff up, that he sort of knew where his dad kept the spare credit cards various companies sent him – an extra Visa, you know, just in case he got bored with using Mastercard – and he felt guilty just thinking what that meant. It meant, if he could get his hands on one of them, that he'd be able to buy a ticket to Tokyo . . .

He spent the rest of the afternoon taking the thought through to various conclusions, all of which lived or died on the basis that his dad hadn't decided to do the sensible thing and cut the cards up and thrown them away. Which he could well have done. But if he hadn't, Adam couldn't see *that* many reasons why he shouldn't get away with it, at least until the bill came through a few weeks later. By which time he could've found Charlie and then everything would look very different.

Pacing up and down in his room made him feel like a trapped animal, so he took the idea out for a walk to see if he could get any further with it, spot any really gaping holes in the plan, work out whether it was actually possible or just an empty, ridiculous hope.

After walking for what seemed like ages, Adam found himself coming along the covered pathway that would lead him out of the park on to the high street. Lost in thought and operating on auto-pilot, he'd done the exact opposite of what he'd intended to do, which was not to go anywhere near the places people hung out during the weekend. And up ahead was the reason why. Two of Steve Apperly's friends, with some other guys, coming his way and looking like trouble.

With no Deputy Heads or Games Masters around, there

were only two logical options: turn round and walk away, or run like shit. Option Two seemed the most likely to work in his favour and, as he took off up the path, back the way he'd come, he tried to work out the best way of losing the wolf pack behind him and getting home unscathed. It wasn't going to be easy. The park was pretty much open territory, with the odd stand of trees and not much else in the way of places to hide; it looked like he was going to have to rely on speed and hope for the best.

Then Adam remembered the garden centre.

It was fairly near, it was always full of people and there was a back way out. All he had to do was get there. Behind him he could hear the five chasers gaining on him and he risked a glance over his shoulder, which confirmed that the nearest was only about twenty metres away, with the others fanning out on either side in case he made a move left or right. Not looking good.

Skidding round a sharp right-hand bend, grabbing hold of a metal signpost to aid a quicker turn, Adam powered down the slip road leading to the garden centre and pelted through a narrow gap in a thick, shoulder-height hedge between the road and what the company which owned the place liked to call the Nature Zone. Too-lazy-to-mow-zone more like. Ducking down below the hedge, Adam ran in a crouch for about fifty metres, then, as he broke cover and made for the back of the garden centre building, he heard voices – far too close for comfort – shouting, *'There he is!'*

Breathing like a steam train, sweating like he'd just got out of the shower, he zigged through the display of decorative bushes and shrubs (shouldn't there be a Botanic Liberation Front that stopped people making plants look like dolphins?) and zagged in the 'OUT' door by the tills, running past the trolleys loaded with micro-forests of potted vegetation. But where next? It was hard to think straight on the run, but if he remembered the layout of the place correctly he had to get out via the café.

Dodging past clumps of shoppers, keeping as low as he could, Adam ran up the wheelchair-friendly ramp that led to the café and straight through it. As he came out on to the patio area where all the tables were he almost ran back inside – two of the chasers had come round the outside of the building and were closing in on him. But retracing his steps was not going to work. Adam turned and ran between the tables, making for the gateway at the rear of the place and just managing to miss stepping on the tail of a large black dog whose back end was sticking out from underneath a chair.

He was lucky. The two blokes behind him weren't. As Adam pushed open the gate he heard the crash of a tin tray loaded with tea, coffee and cakes hitting the ground, and all hell breaking loose as the man who'd been carrying it had a go at the boy who'd run into him, grabbing hold of his shirt and shouting that he was going to have to pay for what he'd done. One down. Then the second guy, who didn't stop to help his friend, also didn't spot the dog's tail. He must've stamped on it hard because the resulting yelp was loud, angry and agonised, and the dog, still tied to the metal chair, gave snarling chase himself. Chaos.

Adam wished he could've stayed and watched, but there was the small matter of the other people still out there after him. He looked around; somewhere the other side of the maze of greenery, beyond the wall of plastic-bagged earth and gravel and eco-friendly compost, was the back entrance, the one where you came in to pick up your

Christmas trees. God, he hoped it was open, because if they caught him down there he'd have no chance.

His mouth drier than a slice of stale bread, thinking he'd give anything for a glass of cold water, Adam sprinted through the ranks of palm trees, rows of whatever and displays of flowering plants, so electric-bright they looked suspiciously fake. Coming out into the goods area he swore under what breath he had left as he saw the gates were closed. Closed, yes. Locked, no! He ran over and pushed back the heavy latch, dragging the gate towards him just enough so he could slip through; as he did, coming between the palms and young trees, he saw three figures running towards him.

Adam pulled the gate to – no time to try and find something to jam it shut with – and ran for the main road. If they caught him, getting done over by three people was, he supposed, better than getting done over by five of them. Got to look on the bright side. Traffic was heavy going up the hill, but if he could get across it would slow the others down too. And then he saw a bus coming down the other way . . . would his luck hold?

Relying on the kindness of your average car driver is no way to cross a busy road, but Adam had run out of choices and just had chances left. Spotting a marginally bigger gap between an approaching red Fiesta and a silver, old-style Micra, he stared at the white-haired lady Micra driver, waving and pointing at the bus, and stepped into the road.

The gamble paid off as the woman, frowning, slowed down just enough to let Adam get to the middle of the road and then dash between another two cars to the other side. He ran the hundred metres down the hill to the bus stop, watching the three pursuers hovering, pissed off, on the opposite side of the road, trapped by the stream of cars. Panting, he put out his hand and waited for the bus to stop; as the doors hissed open he flashed his travel card and went to sit right at the back.

Without bothering to look round, Adam raised his hand and flicked the finger at the rear window to whoever might be watching. So much for a quiet walk to sort stuff out in his head . . .

10

Joyful impression

After a supper during which no one said much about anything, and, in particular, nothing about Charlie, Adam went
to watch some TV. He was a curious mixture of pumped up,
knackered from all the running and nervous as hell about
what he had to do next.

What he had to do first was just sit tight and wait for his
parents to go to bed, which, judging by what they'd been
like over the last week, wouldn't be too long. There was
nothing much on any of the channels; films had either started or weren't anything he wanted to watch, there was no
comedy, no crime, no cartoons. Rubbish.

He got up and flicked through the small collection of
DVDs they'd got, but, as they'd mostly been acquired by his
mum, there was nothing remotely interesting there. Which
left the videos. There were five packed shelves of them,
going back God knew how many years, and, looking at the
dust, most of them hadn't been out of their cases for ages.
It was like being in a cellar looking at a collection of fine
wines, as quite a few of the films had been taped off the TV
and had handwritten labels on the spine – ah, *Wayne's
World*, Aug '99, a very good year for laughs . . .

It was odd how videos, once the total business, were now

kind of antique, like music cassettes. Adam finally picked up *Duck Soup*, Charlie's favourite Marx Brothers movie, thinking that he couldn't remember the last time he'd used his Walkman – probably not since the previous year, when he'd got an mp3 player for a combined birthday/Christmas present.

It took Adam a good twenty minutes hunting to discover the remote tidied away in the cupboard where his mother kept a huge amount of assorted family snapshots, in no particular order, along with the bottles of drink – the orange liqueurs and other odd-coloured, strange-smelling liquids – that no one touched unless everything drinkable had run out. Logical. Where else would you put a remote?

He'd just settled down and was fast-forwarding to the film when his mum popped her head round the door.

'We're off to bed . . . everything all right?'

'Yeah, Mum, fine.'

'What are you watching?'

'*Duck Soup*,' Adam replied without thinking, instantly regretting not having hit 'pause' and made something up. He watched the tears well up in his mum's eyes as she stood, watching the title sequence of the movie. He stopped the tape and got up. 'Don't, Mum . . . please don't . . . I'm sorry, I shouldn't have . . .'

'It's not your fault. I can't help it, Adam . . . I think about her every waking minute and when I'm asleep I dream about her, too. I think I'm going mad, not knowing what's happened. And then . . . and then there's your gran . . .'

Adam, taller than his mum by a couple of inches, put his arms round her and felt her sag against him, sobbing quietly. He felt so bad that this was what all the doing nothing and the waiting were putting her through; he felt like the parent, holding his mum, patting her back and telling her it was going to be OK. But this wasn't about falling over and hurting yourself or some small pet going belly up. He knew it would only be OK if someone did something.

'Try not to worry, Mum . . .'

She looked up at Adam. 'Charlie loved that film.'

'Don't talk like that, she's just missing, like the stupid video remote was missing until I spent some time looking for it . . . she'll be found, Mum, she will.' Adam watched his mum try and smile, leant down slightly so she could kiss him goodnight and watched her go out of the room. He wondered how parents felt when they lied to their children – *it's OK, darling, little Hammy Hamster has gone to rodent heaven . . . you fell over? Let me kiss it and make it better . . . let's roll up your sleeve; no, the doctor's not going to hurt you . . .*

So much bullshit.

The film had finished half an hour ago, but Adam was still watching TV. Giving his eyes something to do while he thought this whole thing through one more time. Or two or three more times, however many it needed until he was satisfied the risks were worth taking.

One floor up, in the room his dad used as a study, there was a freestanding drawer unit. Third drawer down, under some papers, there should be an envelope, a white one with one of those cellophane windows. In the envelope was an unsigned Visa card, valid for another four years, with the name A. T. Grey stamped into it. His dad was Anthony Thomas, he was Adam Thomas. Same middle name. Some family tradition, same initials. He knew he shouldn't have poked around in his father's private things, but he'd been looking for a stapler or hole-punch one afternoon when there was no one else in the house and one thing had led to another.

With the Visa card he could go online and buy a ticket. He'd got a valid passport, he'd got a couple of hundred pounds in a savings account that he could use for expenses – his contribution to this mission – and he'd leave a note for his parents, saying he needed some space and had gone away with Suzy for a few days. No details, no explanation. Much the best way to do it.

Adam still didn't move from the sofa. His parents must've been asleep for well over an hour, and now was the time to set the plan in motion. He chewed his lip, watching an old Cure video, 'Love Cats', on VH1. Taking the card wasn't a problem, he could always put it back, but using it was where he would step right over the line. It was the memory of his mum's face, of holding her as she cried for Charlie, that did it. He jabbed the off button on the cable remote and stood up.

The house was quiet, which meant every move seemed to make a disproportionately loud noise – stairs creaked, door hinges complained, drawers squealed like a pin had been stuck in them. But he finally had the card in his hand. Sitting in the dark study on his father's slightly threadbare office chair, Adam turned the card towards the window and looked at it in the streetlight. He was just about to get up when he thought he heard a noise outside on the stairs.

Shit. Was someone up? Could one of his parents be going to the bathroom, or downstairs to get a glass of water, or whatever it was the way-over-40s did in the middle of the night? Luckily he hadn't turned the light on or he'd be in deep shit.

Eyes fixed on the door, Adam was considering ducking under the desk when he saw a black shadow appear on the landing outside. Badger. 'Bastard . . .' he whispered, finally breathing out. Badger took this to be a perfectly normal greeting and came into the room, tail wagging like he hadn't seen Adam for days.

The dog trotted over and put his cold, wet nose under Adam's left hand, expertly moving it into position so that he kind of had to tickle his ear. Absentmindedly Adam did what was expected of him as he scanned the desk and the drawer cabinet to make sure he'd left everything as it should be. Not that he imagined his father was going to come in and, James Bond-style, check that foreign agents hadn't been at work overnight, but there was no sense in being sloppy.

He and Badger left the study and the two of them went up to his room. Partners in crime.

Adam spent the next hour checking the Net for the best flight deals to Tokyo. He wanted to go as soon as possible, and that meant there were no advanced booking deals to be had. Whatever. He'd have to pay – his dad would have to pay – what it cost. Was £400 a lot to try and find out what had happened to Charlie? He'd no doubt find out when his dad got the bill.

The best flight he could get seemed to be Virgin, leaving Heathrow at 1 p.m. on Tuesday and arriving in Tokyo twelve hours later at 9 a.m. the next morning. The same flight was available tomorrow, but that would mean getting the tube out to Heathrow by around 9:30 a.m., and give him no time to do anything. Adam selected the Tuesday flight. What about coming back? He got up and went to look at the calendar up on his wall to count out the days; noticing that

Badger had obviously got bored and gone off somewhere else, he pushed his bedroom door to.

Counting off the days, Adam figured that he couldn't stay any longer than ten. That would get him back the weekend before his suspension ended, and if he hadn't come up with something after ten days, more time was not going to help. And whatever happened, good or bad, he could always change his flight and come home sooner. He went back and sat at his desk, entering the details for his return flight, then all the payment information.

Buying the ticket shouldn't set off any alarm bells, but would the use of the Visa make anyone sit up and take notice, or would the transaction simply go through? Only one way to find out. As he clicked the mouse on 'Buy' he heard the door being pushed open. He assumed it was Badger coming back in again, so the voice shocked him rigid.

'You're up late. Everything OK?'

Adam looked up to see his father standing half in and half out of his room, looking bleary-eyed and smiling at him in a puzzled, slightly confused way, obviously not quite awake. The spell that had glued Adam's tongue to the roof of his mouth finally wore off.

'Yeah . . . yeah, everything's, you know, fine, Dad . . .'

The room was laid out so that, from where his father was standing, he couldn't see the computer screen, or the credit card lying on the desk in front of the keyboard. Adam had set things up that way on purpose, because there were times you definitely didn't want someone to walk in and see what you were doing.

His dad came into the room. 'Are you emailing?'

Adam surreptitiously pushed the card under his keyboard

with his left hand while he quickly used the mouse to open Outlook over the top of the travel website page.

'I, um, I couldn't sleep . . . I was writing something to Charlie . . .' An easy lie, because it had truth at its core. 'I do it quite a lot.'

His dad sat down on the corner of Adam's unmade bed, yawning. 'I, uh . . .'

'What?'

'I don't know. I suppose I wanted to say, y'know, sorry if I've been an arsehole lately . . .'

'No, Dad, you haven't . . .'

'Yeah, I have, but I feel like I'm trapped. I shouldn't be here, I should be in Tokyo looking for Charlie, but I can't leave your mum, not with Grangie like she is and Granpa Eddy coping so badly.'

'Is Grangie, like, really bad?'

'Pretty much . . . the doctors say that she should go into a hospice, give Eddy some rest.'

'A hospice? Why?'

'Everything's shutting down, Adam. It's only a matter of time. She should be somewhere where they can make her as comfortable as possible.'

Adam felt his stomach knot and his throat tighten, the silence surrounding him and his father becoming almost a physical thing. He couldn't think, didn't know what to say or do, knowing only that he really didn't want to deal with all this shit at the same time.

His father took a deep breath and stood up. 'Hopefully we'll know something very soon, though . . . about Charlie. I had a call from the Foreign and Commonwealth Office on Friday.'

'You didn't tell me – what did they say?'

'Nothing much, they just wanted to assure us that everything that *can* be done to find Charlie *is* being done . . .' A pained expression spread over his dad's face, making him look old and sad and angry. 'Usual Whitehall bollocks. I am going to go . . .'

His father yawned again and for a moment Adam thought he was about to say he was going to Tokyo.

'. . . I'm going to see them tomorrow, get them to tell me what's *really* going on.' He looked at his watch, which wasn't there, and then he glanced over at Adam's wrist. 'I'm off. See you in the morning.'

'OK . . .' Adam wanted to call him back and tell him he understood why he hadn't already gone to Tokyo, why he had to stay and wait to hear what other people were doing instead of doing something himself. But he didn't. He watched his father walk away. '. . . see you tomorrow, Dad.'

11

We produce it for whole human beings

As soon as he woke up, Adam texted Suzy and arranged to meet her later that afternoon. He had to tell her what he was doing – and hope she wouldn't mind that he'd sort of made her a part of his plan. He'd assumed there wouldn't be a problem, because she wouldn't actually have to do anything, but you had to ask. Having successfully kept Suzy a complete mystery to his parents – they didn't even know her first name, let alone any other details – there was a good possibility she wouldn't be involved at all.

Adam also realised that, since changing schools at the end of Year 7, he'd also changed almost all his friends, and while his parents knew his present social circle reasonably well, they didn't socialise with his friends' parents, not like they'd used to when he was at junior school. If, for what-ever reason, they tried to find out where he had gone with this nameless girlfriend of his, there was no way they'd be able to just pick up the phone and do it.

Before he met up with Suzy he had a lot of stuff to get done. A lot of stress to deal with. Starting with actually find-ing where he'd put his passport. It was nowhere to be found. Abso-lute-ly-no-where. Adam turned his room upside down, tidied everything back up, kind of, and then looked everywhere again. Twice. Nothing. He thought hard, trying to remember the last time he'd used it. It was the long weekend trip he and a couple of mates had taken to Amsterdam during the previous autumn break. And then he remembered. It would be where his mum always kept the family's passports, ever since he was a kid. In her bedside cabinet. She must've found it when she emptied his bag and did his washing.

By four o'clock, when he'd agreed to meet Suzy at a café just off the high street, Adam had got his money – £150 in traveller's cheques and £75 in Yen, which cleaned him out, but what the hell – he'd bought the *Rough Guide to Tokyo*, some toothpaste, deodorant, batteries, shampoo and a new pair of sunglasses. The bare essentials. He also had a new battery put in his old Casio watch – it could show dual time, which he was sure would be useful. At home, after checking the weather in Tokyo again – hot and humid – he'd gathered together the minimum amount of clothing he reckoned he could get away with and had found a mid-sized backpack, hidden at the bottom of Charlie's closet, that he was sure he could jam everything into.

Every time he completed a task, ticking it off on his mental list, he felt good, but then when he did something major, like rinse his savings account, he felt sick with an awful mix of guilt and heightened anticipation; the emotional cocktail swung him first down into the depths of self-loathing, because he was doing all this behind his parents' backs, and then way back up in the clouds. He was going to Tokyo. He was going to find Charlie. He really was.

Suzy, already waiting for him, smiled as he walked into

the café. 'You look pleased with yourself, anything happened?'

Adam leant over and kissed her. 'You could say.'

'Could say what?'

'You're probably gonna think I'm crazy, but I'm going to Tokyo.'

Suzy's eyes widened. 'With your dad, to try and find Charlie? That's great, Ad!'

Adam pulled out a chair and sat down. 'By myself . . . I'm going by myself.' Now he'd said it out loud for the first time, to another person. Waiting for Suzy's reaction, he felt like Wile E. Coyote when he'd careered off the cliff in pursuit of the Roadrunner and was hanging in midair, waiting to plummet way, way down into the canyon. 'Told you it was crazy . . .'

'But why . . . ?'

'I can't stand watching my mum cry all the time because she doesn't know what's going on with Charlie.' Adam sat back and watched a man at another table light up a ciga-rette. 'And I can't stand waiting for the time to be right for my dad to go. So *I'm* doing it. Going tomorrow.'

'Tomorrow?'

'Yeah, one o'clock flight from Heathrow.'

'Where'd you get the money, Ad?'

'You really don't want to know . . . but I need your help.'

'To do what?'

'I'm going to leave a note saying that we've gone away for a few days . . . you don't have to do anything – and they don't know how to get in touch with you – but don't tell anyone where I am, not even Andy.' Adam could smell the cigarette, could almost feel the chemical reaction as he breathed it in; smell it, want it, like when you went past a fast-food restaurant.

'You shouldn't't've told me then, should you? Cos if you hadn't, then I really wouldn't know.'

Adam frowned; there she was, being practical again. 'I had to tell someone, Suze . . . I've been inside my head with it all since last night and had to run it past someone.'

'You normally run something past a person *before* you do it.'

'OK, so I said it wrong, sorree . . .' Adam got up, not looking at her. 'You want a cup of coffee?'

'Coke?'

'OK.'

This was not how he'd wanted it to be. He wouldn't see Suzy again till he got back from Tokyo and he needed to know she was with him on this, really behind the idea. He took their drinks back to the table and sat down.

Suzy reached over and took Adam's hand. 'I always say the wrong things, don't I?'

'Not always.'

'Often, I know I do.'

'Sometimes.'

'You expect something, a reaction, and I don't know what it is.'

'What it is now is that I don't want to end this with an argument.'

'End what?'

'This, here. End up going home and off to Tokyo.'

'I do care, Ad.'

'Yeah, I know you do, you just have a weird way of showing it sometimes.'

They sat in an awkward silence for a moment or two, neither quite sure where things were heading, then Suzy poured the last of the Coke into her glass. 'I won't say anything, promise . . . but are you sure this is the right thing to do?'

'Gotta do something, Suze, make an effort.' Adam took a deep, deep breath. 'My house, it's like we're all waiting for the axe to fall, for the call that . . .' He stopped, like something was stuck in his throat.

'That what, Ad?'

'They think she's dead, like that other girl . . . my mum's already talking about her like she's not coming back, it's like she's given up without trying. She can't help it, Suze, my gran's dying and my granpa's gone into meltdown, too. So *I'm* going to bloody go and try to find her.'

'But if you disappear, won't that completely freak your parents? I mean *both* of you gone – and your grandparents? Sounds like that could really do your mum in.'

'I won't've disappeared, Suze, just gone away . . . I'll be with you, right? Just away somewhere.' Adam looked at Suzy looking back at him and he knew she'd realised he was making this up as he went along. 'If I'm away for a while I'll ring them, let them know I'm OK . . .'

'How long d'you think you'll be away?'

Adam measured a spoonful of sugar into his now almost frothless, tepid cappuccino and stirred it. 'Back Friday after next, at the latest.'

'Where are you staying?'

Adam stopped stirring. Where was he staying? All he'd thought about was getting himself to Tokyo, not really any further than that.

'I, uh . . . I was gonna sort that out when I got there.'

Suzy shook her head, smiling at him. 'Capsule hotels.'

'What?'

'I read it in a magazine. In Tokyo they have these kind of

pods, sort of plastic boxes stacked one on top of another? You sleep in them, one person per pod. They're called capsule hotels and the article said they have them by the main stations, for people who're too wrecked to get home.'

'That right?' Adam grinned back at Suzy, thinking that sometimes being practical had its advantages.

Suzy smiled back. 'Absolute fact. Want to come back to my pod?'

12

Fooding space

Most mornings his parents were out of the house by eight thirty, at the latest. You could just about set your watch by them. But this last week everything had been shot to hell, no rhythm, no familiar pattern. In some godawful practical demonstration of Sod's Law it was ten past nine and, while his dad had left, his mother *still* hadn't gone. With her in the house, he was not going to be able to swan out of the front door with a stuffed backpack without her asking him at least a couple of questions he'd find hard to answer. Lying to his mum was not something Adam had ever been very good at.

He should be able to just waltz downstairs and ask her nonchalantly how come she was still at home. It'd be the most natural thing to do, engage her in conversation, find out if she was going off to see her parents or whatever. But he did not feel at all nonchalant; his bag was packed and he'd already checked he'd got his money, passport, credit card and e-ticket at least three times. He was not relaxed. The note he'd written, explaining that he was going away with Suzy – no names, just referring to her as 'his girlfriend' – was sealed up in an envelope, waiting to be left on the dresser in the hall. There was nothing left to do but leave;

he was ready to go, he was on a schedule, and he was trapped in his room.

Adam paced up and down and waited for the tell-tale sound of the front door closing and his mum's car starting up. What was she doing? Why didn't she go? If she'd decided to stay at home all day – which, as she'd taken compassionate leave from work because of Charlie and Grangie, could well be the case – what the hell was he going to do? He was building up such a nice head of stressed-out steam that he didn't hear his name being called until it was accompanied by a rap on his door.

'Are you there, Adam?'

His head snapped round at the sound of his mother's voice – kee-ryst, she was going to come in and see his bloody backpack!

'Yeah . . . sure . . .' He kicked the bag under his desk and sat down, as if he was working on the computer. 'What is it?'

The door opened. 'You must've been miles away, I was calling from downstairs.'

'Sorry.' Adam nodded at the computer screen, feeling his face flush. 'I was thinking about the stuff I've got to do for college. Did you want something?'

'Just to say goodbye.'

'OK, Mum, see you later.'

'Are you all right?' His mother came into the room and walked over towards where he was sitting. 'You look, I don't know, nervous.'

Adam stood up and moved away from the desk. 'No, I'm fine . . . it must be, you know, everything that's going on.'

His mum smiled, a pale imitation of her normal full-beam grin. 'Come here.' She put her arms around him and gave him a hug. 'Your dad's gone to the Foreign Office today to find out what's been happening, what the Japanese police have been doing.' She stood back, sniffing, blinking her eyes and not looking directly at him. 'I'll call you as soon as, um, as soon as I know anything, promise.'

'OK, Mum, hope . . . you know, hope everything's OK.'

'Me too.' she turned to go. 'Work hard . . .'

Adam waited a good ten minutes, just in case his mum was still in the area, and then belted out of the house. He was a couple of houses down the road when he remembered he had neither double-locked the front door nor left the letter on the dresser. Cursing his dullard stupidity, he stormed back, unlocked the door, hauled the envelope out of his backpack, put it at eye level on one of the dresser shelves and was back out of the door, slamming it behind him, in seconds.

What he couldn't know was that, when he slammed the door, the envelope fell off the shelf and landed face down on top of a pile of postal detritus that only ever got looked at when it appeared likely to topple over. Later that evening, when his parents came home, his father would put the first of many pieces of junk mail on top of it.

The tube was the cheapest way out to Heathrow, but it was a long, long ride with plenty of time to think about what he was doing, plenty of opportunity to change his mind. Once he'd got on to the Piccadilly line at King's Cross it was twenty-six stops before he'd arrive at his destination. Twenty-six chances to get off and take the next train back home.

Approaching Knightsbridge was the first time he got it bad. The panic attack – that what he was doing was foolish, ridiculous, a totally crap idea – gave him the sweats, but he sat through South Ken and Gloucester Road and by the time the train stopped at Earl's Court he was back in charge. So what if it was foolish, ridiculous and crap? It wasn't *wrong*, and that, in the end, was what counted.

As the tube pulled into Northfields, with only eight stations to go, Adam felt the tension building again. He was about to get on a plane and fly who knew how many thousands of miles to a place where he knew no one – didn't even know where he was going to *stay*, for chrissake – and basically go missing. What if his parents didn't buy into the idea that he'd buggered off with his girlfriend (who they didn't know) and they freaked out? He'd just be causing them more hassle and heartache.

At Hounslow West he actually got up, ready to exit the train, determined that he was going to catch the next eastbound tube, but as the doors opened he remembered his mum's face, remembered that part of her was beginning to believe Charlie was dead, and the fact that all his dad had been able to do so far was visit the Foreign Office. He'd sat back down before the doors had closed and he stayed where he was until the train rolled to a halt at the Heathrow Terminals 1, 2 and 3 stop. This was it.

Adam thought, as he got off the train and started the walk up to the check-in desks, that his mind was made up. No more backtracking, he was going to go to Tokyo. But then he checked his watch, again, saw he actually still had fifteen minutes till he *had* to check-in and found himself veering off to a coffee shop and ordering a cappuccino he didn't really want. What he wanted was fifteen more minutes' grace, until there were no more chances to change his mind. As soon as his backpack was tagged and checked in, his last exit would absolutely and finally be closed.

Next stop would be passport control, then X-ray, then airside.

He sat on a high stool at a small, round table and watched the ebb and flow of people, like ants in a nest, all with destinations, all with reasons of their own why they were here. Some were probably running away – without telling anybody where they were going – from something or someone; others were possibly going off to begin a new life, maybe even in a place they'd never been to before, but he doubted any of the people he was watching were as alone as he was right then. He even allowed himself to admit that he was scared and, having let that thought loose, he was puzzled but happy to find that he felt better now he no longer had to physically make himself ignore the fact.

At five minutes to eleven he got up, left his hardly touched coffee and walked towards the snaking queue that would take him inexorably to one of the ladies sitting under a sign announcing Virgin Atlantic VS900 Tokyo.

'Is that it, sir, one item of luggage?'

'And this.' Adam held up the small bag he'd brought with him; while waiting in the queue, he'd taken it out of his backpack and loaded it with his mp3 player, sunglasses, spare batteries, passport, e-ticket, money and the Rough Guide.

'Fine, sir.' The woman smiled. 'Did you pack this bag your-self?' Adam nodded. 'Was it out of your sight at any time?' Adam shook his head. 'Did anyone give you anything to take with you?'

'No, nothing.'

The woman printed out a baggage ticket, attached it to the backpack and then sent it off into the bowels of Heathrow. Adam realised the next time he saw it he'd be in Japan. Still sweaty-palmed from when he'd had to hand over the credit card he'd used to pay for the ticket online – the check-in lady had hardly glanced at it – his stomach now felt like it was a negative space, like everything had been sucked out of it.

'Flight's quite full, sir, but you can have the choice of a couple of window seats.' The woman checked the screen in front of her. 'They're near the back, or I have a few of aisle seats further towards the wing. Otherwise it's going to be a middle seat in the centre section – do you have a preference?'

Adam hadn't flown that much, but whenever he'd had a window seat he'd always felt hemmed in, any advantage gained by having a view lost because you had no freedom of movement.

'An aisle seat, please.'

The woman tapped a few keys on a keyboard he couldn't see, waited a moment or two and then, smiling, handed Adam his passport, e-documentation and a card folder with his outbound docket and seat number.

'Have a good flight, and enjoy your stay in Japan, sir.'

Five minutes later he was sitting down at a café in the departure lounge with a hot panini and another coffee. While he waited for the toasted sandwich to cool down Adam texted Suzy that he was at the airport and to text him when she got out of her Spanish tutorial. Then he sat back, relaxed for the first time since he'd woken up that morning.

Now he was on the move, now the only way he could go was forward and, one way or another, he would find out what had happened to Charlie. He would do that.

He didn't care how much trouble he was going to be in, and he knew, no matter what happened, he was going to be in some deep, deep shit when he got home. The feeling that he was doing something, that he was the one who'd got up off his arse and gone for it, was worth whatever they might throw at him. Adam picked up the panini, blew on it and took a bite. Which was when his phone started to ring.

He checked the screen: Suzy. He flipped the phone open. 'Hi.'

'Where are you?'

'Departure lounge.'

'What're you doing?'

'Lounging.'

'Ha-ha . . . has your gate come up yet?'

Adam looked over at the nearest screen. 'Nope, still "Wait in lounge".'

'Why d'you sound odd?'

'Mouthful of food, I was starving . . . couldn't eat breakfast this morning, my mum didn't leave the house till twenty past nine.'

'Are you OK?'

'As good as it gets.'

'Promise you'll email when you get there . . . they have to have Internet cafés there, right?'

'You'd think . . . I'll check in the guidebook, I've got plenty of time to read it.' Out of the corner of his eye Adam saw the lines of text on the screen hanging down from the ceiling flicker and change; he focused on the display. 'Got a gate number, Suze.'

'Be careful, Ad, *please* be careful . . .'

'I'm not going to be acting like some stupid superhero or anything . . .'

'Be back soon . . .'

Adam could hear Suzy's voice breaking. 'Don't cry, Suze . . .'

'I love you.' Click. Silence.

Adam sat, phone still open, connected to nothing. She'd never said she loved him before. Not like that. Weird thing was, he realised he had no idea what he would have replied if she hadn't cut the call.

13

I may be passed if you are speednuts

Adam was surprised to find that a lot of the Virgin cabin crew were Japanese, not English. As he walked through the plane to his seat he found himself being politely welcomed, smiled at and bowed to, and by the time he'd sat down he felt he was already in a foreign country.

He had certainly never flown in this kind of plane before. Even back in cattle class each seat had its own TV screen and hand-held remote/games handset – what the hell did you get up in first class? – and like the check-in lady had said, almost every seat was taken. It seemed as if the majority of passengers were Japanese tourists on their way home; Adam watched smartly dressed middle-aged Japanese ladies, all cream silk, pearls and cashmere, hurrying up and down the aisles armed with clip boards and biros, fussing like mother hens as they checked off 'their' people.

And then the serious stuff began to happen: overhead lockers were closed, seatbelts were checked, hand luggage stowed, and final warnings given about turning off mobile phones and other electrical equipment. Take-off was imminent. His mission was ready for go.

Nothing he could do now but watch movies and eat food.

Sarah Grey got home just after six p.m., glad to find that Adam had remembered to double-lock the front door and wondering if he'd managed to lock up at the back. Teenage boys appeared to have brains capable of concentrating for what seemed like days on computer games, but were totally incapable of remembering the small but important things in life. Like basic home security or flushing the toilet.

As she pushed the door open Sarah could feel there was post behind it, but she was in a hurry; Dave and Jess were coming round for dinner, which she hadn't even begun to prepare, and Tony could pick the post up when he got back. You never knew, Adam might do it if he came home first. As she walked down the hall the last thought almost made her laugh.

Dave and Jess, two of their oldest, closest friends, had suggested the four of them meet up and go out for a meal. But Sarah knew that with the way she felt, preparing and cooking food – actually *doing* something – would distract her. It would keep her mind off Charlie, off her mother's slow, inexorable plummet into dementia and the picture in her head of her dad wandering through their house like a lost soul, if only for a short time. Sarah had decided to cook something she hadn't done before so she'd really have to concentrate: a Thai green curry, from scratch, no packets, nothing prepared.

Unpacking the three carrier bags she'd brought in from the car she had a momentary panic that there wasn't enough food, that she'd forgotten to include Adam in her calculations – but there was, and she hadn't. Anyway, he probably wouldn't be home when they ate, or even eat with them if he was, but she liked to have food there for him when he wanted it. Tony thought she mollycoddled Adam and she knew she probably did, a bit, but why not? He wasn't going to be living with them for ever.

In the end, after a couple of tricky moments, the meal had turned out to be pretty good, if she did say so herself. Even the rice, and Sarah was not known for being good at rice. Delicious though the food was, the main focus of the evening was not on the quality of her culinary skills. It was inevitable that just about all they'd talked about was Charlie – what else, under the circumstances, was there to do: discuss house prices?

The fact was, when Charlie wasn't the topic of conversation, it was ageing, terminal parents they talked about. Sarah had known that that was how the evening was going to go, and had had no desire to get emotionally shredded in public. Bursting into tears in front of friends, ones like David and Jess who cared and understood, was absolutely fine – it was a huge relief being able to talk to people who didn't just nod at you sympathetically – but it wasn't something she could do in a restaurant.

After the weeping and the food and tears, Tony brought Dave and Jess up to speed with what he'd been told at the Foreign and Commonwealth Office, which, when you added it all up, didn't amount to much; the police, through Interpol, had contacted the Tokyo police authorities, and the FCO had contacted the UK embassy in Tokyo, who would, in turn, be getting in touch with all the consulates in other cities. The investigation into Charlie's disappearance would apparently be handled entirely by the Japanese police, who, the FCO official had said, were unlikely to ask for help as their resources were more than adequate. They would, said the official, have to be patient. It had only been a week.

Only a week? ONLY A WEEK! Sarah had been furious when Tony, ringing from outside the FCO, had told her what the official had said. Bloody woman! There was no way on this earth she could have any kids of her own, but if for some bizarre, twisted reason she did, God help them. When Tony repeated that part of the story Sarah couldn't stop the tears, hot and silent, from cascading down her cheeks again. Jess, holding her, cried too, and it was a relief all over again to shed the bottled-up emotions she'd been carrying round all day.

'Did they say anything about whether you should go out there, Tony?' Dave sat back after filling up their wine glasses.

'Entirely up to us whether we do or not.' Tony looked over at Sarah. 'We've talked about it, haven't we,' Sarah nodded, biting her lower lip, 'and there's no way Sarah can go, with her mum and dad and everything, and *I* can't leave her to cope with that situation on her own . . . no way, right?'

The question stayed, waiting for someone, anyone, to answer it.

Tony frowned. 'What're you saying, Dave? That I should've gone?'

Dave shook his head, leaning forward, elbows on the table. 'Not saying that, Tony, mate . . . course not, I just can't get my head round what a bastard it is to have to make that sort of decision. And anyway, when you see people who have gone to try and help find someone who's missing, they don't seem to do anything much except provide news programmes with thirty seconds of film of them standing in some street, and a sound bite.'

Sarah blew her nose. 'Did you phone that detective, Tony, the one who came here when we first reported Charlie missing?'

'Venner?' Tony took a drink. 'Yeah, I did . . . he said he'd do some chasing, but like they said at the Foreign Office, all police contact has to be through Interpol. He said he'd call me tomorrow. Have you given up smoking, Dave?'

'Why?'

'Because if you haven't, I would like one.'

'Tony!' Sarah frowned. 'Don't do it, don't start again, if Adam sees you smoking – he said one of the reasons he'd stopped was because if you could, so could he.'

'The discussion is moot, I have no fags.' Dave nodded at his wife. 'Nurse Ratchet over there would have my guts for garters if she even suspected I'd thought about buying a packet. Talking of Adam, how's he taking all this?'

Sarah looked over at Tony. 'Not particularly well . . . he got suspended for two weeks because he got into a fight at college. Some stupid boy making off-colour remarks about what Charlie was doing in Tokyo. He took it very personally. Broke the boy's finger.'

'He said it was a mistake, Sarah! What would you rather he did, let them say whatever they like about his sister?'

'I'd actually rather we didn't have an argument, not now . . .'

Dave and Jess left just before midnight, Sarah insisting she didn't want any help with the clearing up. Back in the kitchen Tony, loading the dishwasher, apologised for losing his rag about Adam.

'Where is he, anyway – did you see him today?'

'This morning, just before I left to go to Mum and Dad's.'

'How was he?'

'He was . . . he was OK.'

Tony looked up from arranging the dirty plates in ascending order of size. 'What was the matter with him?'

'Oh, I don't know . . .' Sarah wiped an already clean work surface. 'He wasn't himself, you know?'

'None of us are, right now. D'you think he's coming back tonight?'

'Or staying with The Girlfriend? I've no idea, given up asking. Do you think we'll ever get to meet her?'

Tony stood up. 'Does she even exist?'

'Oh, yes!'

'Mother's intuition?'

'No, smelt the perfume, seen the lipstick – I'm not saying where – and I think her name's Suzy.'

'How d'you know that?'

'Saw a piece of paper on his desk, covered with her name. You know, the way you do when you first fall for someone? Remember?'

'Were you spying?'

'Nothing so underhand, just getting his dirty laundry . . .'

Adam looked at his watch, which was still on UK time. It was twenty to midnight, which meant . . . He'd forgotten what the time difference was, disoriented from a combination of snacking, watching too many movies and not sleeping enough. He looked up and down the aisle, spotted the hostess – Takako, if he'd remembered it right – who'd been looking after his section and got up to go and speak to her. She'd know what the time was in Tokyo.

He stretched, his cramped muscles complaining about being stuck in virtually the same position for hours on end, observing the hushed compartment full of people sleeping, reading, eating, engrossed in movies, some even talking to each other. All at 30,000 feet. He walked down the aisle to the station at the rear of the plane where the food and drink was stored and found Takako finishing a glass of water.

'Hi, I um, could you . . .' He showed her his watch. 'I haven't changed this yet . . . what's the time in Tokyo?'

Takako smiled. 'It's twenty to eight, in morning. We'll be landing around hour and half.'

He took his watch off and fiddled with the buttons to change the time in the watch's second zone; it was now Wednesday, had been for hours. 'What's it like?'

'Tokyo?'

'Yeah . . . is that where you come from?'

Takako nodded. 'But I live in London now, since I start flying . . . Your first time in Japan? On holiday?'

Adam's turn to nod. 'Sort of . . . my sister's out there.' Adam didn't think this was the time to go into details about exactly what he was going to be doing in Japan. 'What's the best way to get in from the airport? Doesn't look too far on the map, is there an underground, like at Heathrow?'

One of the male cabin crew came into the station.

'What would you say, Giichi, the best way to get into Tokyo, train or coach?'

Giichi thought for a moment, then shrugged. 'I think coach? Little bit more expensive, but leave more often maybe.'

'Where are you staying?' Takako smiled, head slightly to one side.

'Can't remember, got the address back at my seat . . . somewhere fairly central I think, near a station.' Suzy had said the capsule hotels were all near mainline stations.

'Probably best get train, then.' Giichi nodded pensively. 'You can get subway to anywhere from Asakusa, easy – plenty of English on the signs!'

'How long are you staying?'

'About ten days.'

'Good time of year, not too hot.' Takako nodded. 'We must get breakfast ready now, sorry.'

'Oh, right, breakfast.' Adam looked at his watch, 'Tokyo time . . . I'll let you get on. Thanks for the advice.'

It was breakfast Japanese-style, with a hot, slightly fishy soup that actually turned out to be made of soy beans, and rice wrapped in dried seaweed. Not a muffin or a croissant in sight. Adam wasn't really hungry, but he tried the rice, just to get in the mood, and didn't particularly like it. After the debris had been cleared away Takako came by and gave him a folded piece of paper.

'What's this?'

'Instructions, just in case.'

'Just in case what?'

'You get lost.' Takako reached over and unfolded the paper and Adam saw she'd written a couple or more English phrases, like 'Which way to the station, please?' with their Japanese translation underneath. 'Have a good trip.'

14

Stay real, be sexy

Adam sat looking at the immigration form in front of him. He'd filled everything in, except where he was staying. Could he write in Capsule Hotel Riverside, or Capsule Land Shibuya? According to the Rough Guide these places were 'generally for one night', so he thought maybe not . . . probably shouldn't. He didn't know how important it was to put down where you were staying, but had heard his dad tell the story about a friend who'd been turned round by immigration at JFK in New York and sent home. He couldn't now remember why, just found himself worrying that it'd happened to someone sort of connected to him. Was that a bad omen?

But then, as he chewed the end of his pen, it slowly dawned on him that he could make it up. Surely they couldn't check where every single visitor stayed, could they? He got the guidebook out of his small backpack again and began leafing through the accommodation section.

Standing in the queue, waiting his turn to be seen by an immigration officer, Adam wondered, if they somehow guessed he was lying about where he was staying, would they really turn him away, send him back home?

Home. His mind flashed on a series of images – his mum and dad . . . Badger . . . Grangie and Granpa Eddy, before, when they were both fine – and it came as a shock that he hadn't thought about any of them since he'd left the house.

He wondered what would happen if his parents had found out what he'd done and had got in touch with the authorities in Tokyo – once they realised who he was would he be hauled out of the queue, handed over to the cops and then put on the first UK flight? Or would –

'Excuse me, it's your turn.'

Adam, feeling a tap on his shoulder, looked up and focused in front of him. He saw that, without realising, he'd moved so far forward he was now first in line and there was an empty bay to his right. He glanced at the man behind him, an American. 'Sorry.'

'It's OK, I'm kind of asleep at the wheel myself.'

Adam went over to where a doll-like woman, hardly visible over the ledge in front of her, was waiting for him to hand over his passport and papers. 'Sorry.'

She nodded without looking at him and began to go through his passport, stopping to check the reality against the photo. 'Grasses.'

Momentarily taken aback by the fact that Japanese people really did totally pronounce their Ls as Rs, Adam smiled to himself, then saw the woman was miming someone taking off a pair of specs. He'd forgotten he had his new sunglasses on. 'Sorry . . .'

The immigration officer was now checking the form he'd filled in on the plane and Adam found he wasn't tired any more as he stared down at the top of the woman's head, willing her not to ask him about where he was staying. He'd chosen a place the book had said was cheap, cheerful and what he could afford. All she had to do was stamp whatever she had to stamp and let him go . . .

'Horiday?'

'What? Oh, yes . . . just a short one.'

Ka-thunk. 'Have nice stay.'

And that was it. No more polite 'sorry's, he was through. He was in Japan and all he had to do now was find Charlie.

It was almost midday by the time he got into Tokyo. He'd decided to get off the train at Asakusa because that's where the guidebook said there was a pretty decent capsule hotel; the only trouble was, he couldn't book in until at least 3:00 p.m.

Three hours before he could crash. Adam stood outside the station in the bright sunshine just letting everything sink in: this street, these people, this city, all so much the same as at home and at the same time so incredibly dissimilar. People streamed by on the pavement, all different, all individual, but all Japanese. As he watched it occurred to him that this wasn't at all like being in Chinatown back home, like he'd imagined it would be.

Here he was the odd man out, the alien, and he couldn't work out if it was simply how tired he was, but, like a waking dream, nothing quite fitted. On the road it was the same story, with cars, trucks and vans driving on the same side of the road as at home, oddly enough, and all mostly makes he knew – but they were models he hadn't seen before, and everywhere he looked, there were bicycles. Even on the pavements. It seemed like everything you could do while walking, the Japanese also did on a bike – phoning, using a parasol, eating – and all the time ringing their bells to alert pedestrians that they should get out of the way, and quick.

Adam realised he hadn't seen another Caucasian face since leaving the train, that here on the street he must stick out; but no one was staring at him, the way you would at a freak, which made him feel he wasn't quite such a stranger. Maybe Japanese politeness didn't allow pointing. Whatever. Adam still wasn't hungry – it was, he reminded himself, three in the morning body-clock UK time – but he thought maybe he ought to pin down where the Capsule Hotel Riverside was before he did anything else.

Using the small map at the back of the guidebook to orient himself, he crossed the street and hoped that would take him in the direction of the river and the road where the hotel was. When he reached the cross street which should, to his left, lead past a water bus pier to a bridge, he was pleased to see that it did. Who said you had to have been a Boy Scout to be able to read maps?

He went over the road and walked down the small side street opposite till he came to a nondescript white structure with a narrow, external staircase running up the side of it. He couldn't read the Japanese sign above him, attached to the outside of the building, but another one on the wall by the stairs, with a large orange arrow on it, was dual language and told him that this was the Capsule Hotel Riverside, with everything he needed to know – when he could check in, when he had to check out and how much it would cost him to stay. He did a quick calculation and thought £15 sounded reasonable enough, although he still had no idea what a room, or rather a capsule, in one of these places looked like. Truthfully, he really didn't care as long as he could – eventually – lie down in it.

Adam turned round and made his way back to the main road. There were still two and a half hours to go before he would be allowed in, so he might as well not waste his time and instead use it to try and figure out a plan of action. He was so tired that he knew there was no point right now in attempting to find the bar where Charlie said she and Alice had been working, but if he bought a bigger map and then found somewhere to sit, a small restaurant or something, then he could get to grips with where everything was and be more up to speed tomorrow morning. The state he was in, it sounded like the best sort of plan he could come up with.

About half an hour later he found a magazine shop; it was a tiny place, packed with more magazines than he'd seen in his entire life. There were magazines on everything you could imagine, right down to the most obscure subject – if you liked dogs you could simply buy *Dog Fan*, but you could also feed your specialist need with a slick, glossy copy of *Dachshund Family*. Luckily, the shop also stocked tourist maps.

It wasn't long afterwards that Adam discovered two things: that he was now getting hungry, and that restaurants in Tokyo made life very easy for you if you spoke no Japanese. Their complete menu was often featured as actual-sized, full-colour plastic models in the window and all you had to do was point. He chose a place that wasn't packed out, pointed at a dish that looked like chicken and rice (and turned out to be exactly that) and sat at a table with his guidebook and new map.

Finally it was three o'clock and he was standing at the bottom of the stairs leading up to the hotel. He took a deep breath, shouldered his backpack and trudged up to the reception on the fourth floor. Walking in he found himself somewhere that was more like the foyer of an old-fashioned gym or swimming pool than a hotel, all polished wood floors and shiny pastel-coloured plastic surfaces, with 50s-style chintzy furniture, a TV and rows of vending machines selling everything – food, fags, soft drinks and beer.

An old man wearing some kind of traditional clothing, like a silk dressing-gown, came out of an office and bowed. '*Konnichi wa.*'

'Hello.' Adam bowed back. The man stood at the reception desk, waiting. 'Oh, right – a room? Please?'

The man nodded and beckoned Adam over to the desk, where he picked up a notice in Japanese and English with the rules of the hotel printed on it. He pointed to the prices, holding out his other hand. Adam handed over a ¥10,000 note, pocketed the change he was given and looked around for the way to get to the rooms.

'Room?' he said, putting his hands together and laying his head on them. The man wrote something on a slip of paper and gave it to him. '8013?'

'*Hai.*' The man pointed upwards, nodding again, holding up eight fingers.

'Eighth floor?'

'*Hai.*'

His shoes were in a small locker downstairs, taken off and stored before he could go up to his floor, his backpack was safely tucked away in a larger locker near the showers, and he'd washed his face and brushed his teeth. Adam looked down the corridor with two tiers of surgical green capsules on either side – basically single-bed width, moulded plastic boxes with disturbingly flesh-coloured interiors. Inside each one was a mattress, pillow, blanket and small television sticking out of the ceiling. No door, just a fabric blind that you pulled down. Home sweet home.

There were no windows anywhere, but at the end of the corridor light spilled in through an open door, and Adam walked down, past his capsule, to have a look outside. Stepping on to the balcony he found beyond the open door, Adam stared first at the massive Asahi beer poster right in front of him, and then down at the wide, calm river. Feeling like he was in some weird alternate reality and this was another Thames, Adam looked at his watch: 3:30 p.m., or 7:30 in the morning back home in London. Right, as his dad still said, 'Time for bed, said Zebedee . . .'

'Tony?'

Silence. Muffled breathing.

'*Tony!*'

'What?'

'He didn't come home last night.'

'Who?'

'Adam, who'd you think?'

'What time is it?'

'Seven thirty-ish.'

Tony rolled over on to his back, rubbed some sleep out of his eyes and looked up at his wife. 'He's stayed out before. He's probably with the girlfriend. Have you tried ringing him?'

'Message service.'

'How long've you been up?' Tony swung his legs over the edge of the bed and stood up, stretching his arms and cracking the knotted muscles in his shoulders.

'Since six. I hate it, Tony.'

'Hate what?'

'Their empty bedrooms. I feel like someone's hit the pause button, Tony.'

The alarm clock started beeping and Tony bent down to turn it off. 'Nothing's on hold . . .'

'It's like they've gone and I never had the chance to say goodbye . . . Charlie, anyway . . . I know Adam's just not here right now, but, you know what I mean.'

Tony wasn't at all sure he did, but nodded anyway, waiting for his brain to get up to speed so he could think of some way of changing the subject.

Sarah went over and drew the curtains. 'What time are you seeing that Detective Sergeant Venner?'

'Nine o'clock. Better get a move on.'

'D'you think we should've gone to Tokyo straight away, as soon as Alice called? And why hasn't she called again? She hasn't even phoned her mother you know. I rang her again yesterday and she told me she still hasn't heard anything from her.'

'You know we couldn't go out there, Sarah.' Tony walked round the bed and put his arms around his wife. 'I feel as out of touch, not connected to all of this as you. I have no idea what we should be doing – there's no helpful guide called "What to Do When Your Daughter Goes Missing in Tokyo" to refer to. Why don't we ask Venner what he thinks?'

'We?' Puzzled, Sarah pulled away and looked up at her husband.

'Come with me. Hear what he's got to say first-hand.'

'But I'm supposed to go over and talk to the people at the hospice . . .'

'They can wait . . . phone them. This is a Charlie day.'

15

It's a labour of human

It was after nine thirty by the time Tony and Sarah found themselves being ushered into an interview room by DC Thomson, the other plain-clothes officer who'd been with Venner when he'd come round to the house.

'DS Venner will be with you in a moment – would either of you like a tea or a coffee? I can't recommend the coffee, but the tea's not bad.'

Tony looked over at Sarah, who shook her head. 'No, nothing thanks.'

Left alone in the room they both sat in silence, looking at the scarred paintwork, at the faded posters taped to the wall and the random collection of flyers and leaflets pinned to the cork noticeboard on the wall.

Sarah got up and stood, her back to the door, looking round the room. 'Know what's weird?

'No, what?'

'I'm forty-five and I've never been inside a police station before. Does that make me some kind of boring goody-goody or what?'

'Some people would say it made you very lucky, Mrs Grey.' Tony and Sarah turned to see DS Venner at the door. 'Apologies for being late, has anyone offered you a drink or anything?'

'We're fine.' Sarah sat back down at the table next to Tony.

Venner pulled out a chair and sat opposite them, put a cardboard file on the table and opened it. 'Right.' He looked up at the pair of expectant faces in front of him. 'To bring you up to speed, I've just checked and there's nothing new in, either via Interpol or direct from the embassy in Tokyo.' Venner saw Sarah's shoulders slump. 'On the positive side, Mrs Grey, we've heard nothing bad.'

Tony reached over for his wife's hand. 'Have you heard anything at all?'

'It's mostly negatives, Mr Grey – Charlotte's not left the country via any major port or airport; there's been no ransom demand, so we can safely assume this is not a kidnap scenario, and no body has been found.' Venner turned a sheet of paper over and read a few lines, looking back up. 'The odd thing is, the Japanese police have been unable to locate either of your daughter's travelling companions to verify the story that Alice Reardon told you over the phone. No sign of her or the male, Steve, whose details we don't have. Do you think there's anything your son might not be telling us?'

Tony frowned. 'Why would you say that?'

'Can't afford to leave a stone unturned, Mr Grey. He knew Charlotte was in Tokyo and never told you, remember? I'm not saying he's definitely withholding information, but I have to address the possibility. With your permission I wouldn't mind having another word with him – what time does he get back from college?'

'He's, ah, not actually *at* college *at* the moment.' Sarah squeezed Tony's hand.

'He's been suspended, Mr Venner. He got into trouble, a fight, protecting his sister's reputation.'

'And we don't know where he is because he didn't come home last night.'

'We know where he was, Sarah, he was with his girlfriend, Suzy . . . wasn't that what you said her name was?' Tony looked at DS Venner. 'We just don't know where *she* lives. They get to an age and you suddenly find you don't know who any of their friends are any more.'

DS Venner closed the file. 'When he does come home, Mr Grey, could you let me know so I can come over and have a word with him?'

'Of course, but I'm sure he's told you everything he knows.'

'It's just my job to make sure he has . . .'

'Do you like him?' Sarah put a sandwich down in front of Tony.

'Who?'

'Detective Sergeant Venner.'

'Like him? I don't know, I hadn't really thought about him like that.'

Neither of them had felt much like doing anything after leaving the police station. No news wasn't always good news, the fact vacuum allowing the frantic side of the imagination to conjure up all the bad things that might have happened. They'd gone home, but Tony was beginning to wonder whether they should maybe just have got in the car and gone for a drive. The house wasn't a particularly relaxing place to be, especially as Adam still hadn't come back.

Tony picked up a sandwich. 'Don't you like him, then, Venner?'

'He was so *suspicious* . . . I mean what else could Adam possibly know?'

'It's his job to be suspicious, it's what he gets paid for, Sarah. What kind of detective would he be if he took everything people told him at face value? I don't think Adam's *up* to anything, but I can see that, under the circumstances, Venner'd want another word.'

'Maybe . . . he wasn't much help about whether it'd do any good, us going to Tokyo, was he?'

'Like he said, it's not his job to give us advice . . .'

'What exactly is his job, then?' Sarah got up, looked at her watch and started pacing the room. 'It's almost one thirty! When is that boy going to come home, Tony? Or even have the courtesy to ring? Does he *ever* pick up his messages? What's the bloody point in having a mobile bloody phone if you don't use the damn thing!'

'Look, you've been up since the crack of dawn, why don't you go and take a nap and I'll –'

'Sleep? Now?'

'Well, just lie down, then, OK? Relax a bit.'

Sarah sat down at the table and began clearing up crumbs. 'What're you going to do?'

'Go to the college and try to find out who this Suzy is.'

Adam woke up with a start, lying still in the semi-darkness, trying to work out where the hell he was. Something, a noise, must've dragged him out of a deep, deep sleep because nothing in his head seemed to be working very efficiently. He rolled over on to his back and his elbow banged on to something hard; he touched it: plastic. Plastic? His eyes finally adjusted to the light level and he remembered where he was. Tokyo. In a box. He pressed the 'light' button on his watch and saw it was 9:30, but whether that was a.m. or p.m. he hadn't the slightest idea.

Toky-oh-my-God . . . it was all Adam could think as he stood in the street, looking at the night-time version of Asakusa going on around him. Then he gazed up at the sky, expecting stars, but in a different pattern to the one he'd see at home.

Nothing. Just black. No stars. Neon all the way.

A whole world of neon. Every colour of the rainbow, except the subtle ones. Flashing on and off, rising and falling like electronic, coloured rain . . . pictures, symbols, graphics, all glowing in the night. And there, among the random, alien light-sprawl, the occasional English words, just to add to the confusion.

PARODY MARKET . . . MY WAY . . . FREE . . . GENIUS AMUSEMENT . . .

Meaningless words trying to make themselves heard amongst the indecipherable visual noise and the cars and the people and the piped music and the conversations. Was everyone here talking to someone else on a mobile phone? It certainly looked that way, with those not talking deeply involved in texting. Adam wondered what a Japanese text message looked like. Very different. Like now. Nothing looked the same as it had during the day and Adam suddenly felt completely disoriented.

'Jeez . . .' What had he done, coming here? How was he ever going to have a chance of finding Charlie in this madhouse – what had he been thinking? He couldn't work out how come it had ever seemed like a good idea, how come Suzy hadn't told him to get real. But she hadn't, he was here and he knew he had to deal with it. Completely his responsibility. As the world flowed around him, it occurred to Adam that he had two choices: go home, the first chance he had, or have a go at doing what he'd come here for.

If he didn't actually make a move, *do* something, he felt like he'd still be standing on this bit of pavement, dithering, when the sun came up. He'd already figured out that the tube map in the guidebook was much harder to make sense of than the one included in the fold-out city map he'd bought; standing in a pool of streetlight he took another look, seeing that he was actually just eleven stops from Roppongi. It could not be that difficult a journey to do, and he'd at least be able to start his search for the Bar Belle and feel he hadn't wasted the whole of his first day in Tokyo.

Underground there was a new world, a bright, clean environment which, considering the neon mayhem going on above it, was astonishingly free of excessive advertising. Working out how to buy a ticket, though, had proved to be no easy job – even after he'd found the button which changed the Japanese characters on the text screen into English. Luckily someone who turned out to understand more English than they actually spoke spotted him standing, dazed and confused, in front of a bank of ticket machines, and between them they'd managed to buy a ticket that Adam hoped would get him to Roppongi and back again.

After the frustrating ticket-buying experience, the journey turned out to be a breeze, just a question of paying attention and following instructions and numbers, of going from A18 to E23, through colour-coded tunnels and on southbound trains. Simple.

Exiting Roppongi station Adam found himself back in Neon City and at what appeared to be a major crossroads. There was an elevated expressway running above one of the streets which had a sign on it in English letting him know he was now in 'High Touch Town', whatever that actually meant. From what the guidebook said, it probably meant what it sounded like. And somewhere here there was a place called the Bar Belle, where Alice and Charlie had been working, and where Alice had last seen Charlie walking out with a customer.

As he had no idea where the girls' apartment was he'd *got* to find the bar. It was the only place to start, the only place he'd be able to hook up with Alice and find out for himself exactly what was going on. Get to talk to Alice's boyfriend, Steve, see what he had to say.

The only problem was he had absolutely no idea where in Roppongi – no small area – to find the Bar Belle. Before leaving England he'd looked it up on the Net, having discovered that a lot of the bars had their own websites, but found nothing. Was it too small? Too scuzzy? Just not bothered? He'd have to find it first to know, but how? Then, above the roar of the traffic, he heard a badly amplified voice calling out, something about beer and girls and music. Now he looked he could see that there were quite a few people, types he recognised from Soho and Brixton, touting various clubs and bars; one of them was using a cardboard megaphone. Most of them were black and one of them might know something. Whether they'd tell him was another matter entirely.

Adam chose the least threatening-looking of the guys and hoped you could judge this particular book by its cover. He approached, friendly, smiling. 'Speak English, man?'

'Chor, wa'choo wan? Nice girl? Cheap booze? We got de bes in town!' All teeth and big smiles, the man thrust a coloured flyer at Adam. 'Jus roun da corner, man, two minutes – you go?'

Adam looked at the piece of paper in his hand: Club Exit. 'No, I'm looking for this place called the Bar Belle, you heard of it?'

'Chor I hear . . . shit place, man, you wan class? You go Exit, man. Lemme take you roun . . .'

'I need to find the Bar Belle, I'm meeting a friend there and I lost the address.'

'Piece a shit place, man.'

Adam dug into his jeans pocket and brought out one of the ¥1,000 notes he'd stuffed in there after buying his subway ticket. 'I really don't care . . .'

The man reached out to take it and Adam moved his hand back. 'OK, right . . . OK, man, see, you go cross da street, you take secon right, you fine it up a few floor, five or six, I don 'member zackly. Look for da sign, man.'

'Thanks.' Adam handed over the note.

It wasn't there. Across the street, second on the right, was a narrow alleyway which restaurants backed on to. It was full of industrial-sized wheelie bins, it smelt of cooking and food and the remains of cleared plates that had sat out in the heat for too long. There was no Bar Belle, not at ground level or five or six floors up, no matter how far down he went. Shit.

Adam turned to go back up the way he'd come, and stopped. Silhouetted against the bright lights of the main drag he saw a figure that seemed to be looking his way, waiting. Double shit. Had he been set up here? More than likely. He looked behind him, back down into the gloom of what looked like a dead end; no point in running down there, then. He cast around in the shadows on the ground for anything he might be able to use to defend himself, and saw nothing.

Walking slowly back up the alley Adam thought about trying to fit some coins between his fingers, make iron knuckles, like he'd seen done in a movie, but he knew he was clutching at straws now. Best just to go for this head on, wait until the last minute and make a rush for the street and hope he got past the guy. He'd be safe out in the crowds. Safer, anyway.

He'd been psyching himself up so much that it was only when he was just about to start running like hell, possibly yelling at the top of his voice, that he realised the person was not only standing with his back to the alley, not looking down it at all, he was also much nearer to the street than he'd realised. And, as the man turned to look to his right, Adam could now see he was quite an old guy.

He feeling of panic subsided, replaced by one of embarrassment as he walked past the man and out on to the pavement; how stupid would he have felt, tearing past this total stranger like a madman? Total dickhead stupid.

Accompanied by an odd sense of anticlimax, Adam made his way back to the big junction and the subway station. He looked at his watch: a quarter to midnight. He didn't know when the trains stopped running, but he'd better not risk missing the last one by hanging round this place much longer; tomorrow he'd come back again and do it properly this time.

As he was about to go down to the trains he saw the tout

standing across the street where he'd left him, still trying to attract the punters. Adam stopped and stared at him, long enough for the man to pick up, the weird way you can do sometimes, that he was being observed. He looked straight across the road at Adam, smiled a yard of teeth and waved. Adam shook his head and went down the stairway, back to his box.

16

Unwept, unhonoured and unsung

You weren't supposed to park in a teacher's space, but it was raining and, quite frankly, thought Tony Grey as he killed the engine, so what. He was trying to hold it all together, but when something like this happened, and nothing in the life you'd led so far gave you any kind of experience to know what you should do or how you should act, it was hard. It was like the first day of your first job, that feeling that whatever you did was bound to be wrong.

He knew Sarah understood how he was feeling, but he didn't know about Adam. Over the last week there'd been a look in his son's eyes sometimes that made him feel weirdly guilty that he wasn't doing enough. Inside he was like a tightly wound spring, waiting to be released, and Adam was old enough, surely, to understand he was jammed solid by the desperate state of affairs with Angie and Eddy. God, whoever wanted to grow old . . .

As he walked round to where he could see students starting to exit the campus site where Adam's sixth form college was, Tony scanned the faces for one he might be familiar with from the old junior school days when Adam still had birthday parties and he knew just about all his friends. Hard as he tried, though, no one rang any kind of bell.

'Hi . . . Mr Grey?'

Tony looked round and saw a boy, about Adam's age, smiling at him. 'Hello . . . do I . . . do I know you?'

'I'm Andy, Andy Cornwell . . . I was at Hillside with Adam?'

'Oh yeah, right. I'm sorry, didn't recognise you.' Tony shook his head. 'It's been a few years, you've all kind of morphed.'

'You're not looking for Adam, are you? Not, you know, here?' Andy looked somehow uneasy.

'I do know he's been suspended, he didn't forget to tell us, but I am looking for Adam. The police want to interview him again, as soon as possible, and he hasn't been home since yesterday. We think he's with his girlfriend — Suzy, is it?' Tony thought he saw the boy almost nod. 'Look, Andy, I know Adam would go ballistic if he thought I'd been up here asking questions about his private life, but it is so private we have no way of getting in touch with him, no idea where he is. Have you seen him?'

'Not since the weekend, actually. Texted him yesterday, but not had a reply.'

'Is Suzy — that is her name, isn't it?' Still no response. 'Is she here? Could you point her out to me? I really do need to talk to him.'

'Is Charlie going to be OK?'

The question took Tony completely by surprise, coming right out of the left field. 'I, uh . . . I think so. I hope so. I don't really know, Andy. I don't know anything, really, nothing at all.' He stopped and breathed in slowly, tamping down the fire inside that made him want to shake this boy and force him to say what he wanted to know. 'Are you going to help me?'

Tony had tried to keep the edge out of his voice, but he knew he hadn't succeeded; he watched Andy move back slightly.

'Help you?'

'You're not ratting anyone out, just helping. Adam isn't in trouble, he's just been in touch with Charlie more than we have, that's all the police want to check on. Maybe there's something she's said that might help find her.'

'OK, look,' Andy glanced round, almost furtively, 'Suzy wasn't in this afternoon. I think she had a revision period.'

'Where does she live?'

'Are you, like gonna go *round* there?'

'I just want to talk to her, Andy. Like I said, no one's in trouble here.' Tony started to tense up again. 'Look, *you* can give me the address, or I can go to the office and get them to tell me. Either way, I am going to find out where she lives. So why not make my difficult life just a *tiny* bit easier, Andy? Can you do that?'

Andy found he that he could provide the address, and that he could also give up Suzy's mobile number and surname as well. Tony felt bad about having played the heavy, but he'd also had it with playing games; he was sure Andy would understand, maybe later, when one of his own kids had disappeared when he or she was halfway round the world.

Sitting in the car, a few yards down from Suzy's house and on the other side of the road, he thought about what to do: phone first or just go and knock on the door? Tony pulled the handle and nudged the door open. Right now the direct approach seemed like the best way forward.

Crossing the road he went up the path and stood in front

of the house, reached to his right and pushed the bell. Somewhere inside, behind the decorative leaded-glass panels, he heard it ringing. Then nothing. Then, faintly, footsteps and through the glass he could just make out the silhouette of a figure coming down the stairs towards him. It looked like a man and Tony found himself wondering, as the door opened, why he'd taken a day off work.

'Mr Barrett?'

The tall, casually dressed man, his chin and head covered in a close crop of silver hair, nodded. 'That's right, how can I help?'

Tony put out his right hand and they shook. 'I'm Tony Grey, Adam's dad.'

'Ah, so he does have parents.' Suzy's father smiled. 'Nice to meet you at last. I'm Chris . . . Sorry to hear about your daughter. It must be terrible.'

Tony ran his fingers through his hair. 'Thanks . . . look, um, is Adam here?'

'Here, now? No, don't think I've seen him for a couple of days. Sorry, rude of me keeping you out there on the step, come in.'

Tony looked at his watch. 'Maybe another time, I have to get back . . . my wife. Is Suzy in?'

'No, she went out after we'd had some lunch, said she was doing revision round at a friend's. Why?'

'We can't get hold of Adam and we need to talk to him – to do with Charlie – and I thought he might be here, or Suzy might know where he was.'

'I'll call her, hang on a tick while I get the phone . . .'

Tony watched Suzy's dad hurry down the hall; he was trapped now, not able to go before he came back. Seconds later he saw him reappear, a cordless phone pressed to one ear, already in conversation; as he got nearer Tony could hear what he was saying.

'. . . I don't exactly know why, they just need to talk to him . . . I also don't know how – is it some big secret where you live? Look, Suzy, if you know something . . . I'm not *accusing* you of anything – and watch your tone of voice, young lady.' Suzy's dad looked up and mouthed 'sorry'. 'Right, come home now. No. I mean it, right now, because you do *not* want me to have to come and get you.'

Tony watched Suzy's dad jab a finger at the phone and put it down on a table which, much like the dresser in his house, was covered in post.

'Don't ask me what that was all about, and I apologise for the scene, but I know my daughter, and she is hiding something . . .'

Suzy had taken the longest twenty minutes to get home and now, sitting at the kitchen table, Tony had to admit she did look as guilty as hell, shifty, nervously picking at a loose thread on her denim bag and seemingly unable to look either of them in the eye. Not the best circumstances under which to meet your son's girlfriend for the first time.

'So,' Suzy's dad put three mugs of freshly brewed coffee on the table and sat down opposite his daughter, 'where is Adam? His parents are already having to deal with their daughter going missing. They don't need any more stress right now.'

Suzy spoke to the tablecloth. 'He said he was going to leave you a note.'

The two fathers exchanged glances and Tony shook his head. 'Where is he, Suzy?'

'I promised not to say anything . . .' Suzy looked up at

her father, chewing her lip. 'Adam said I wouldn't be involved.'

'Well, like it or not, you are, sweetheart.'

Tony could tell the girl's loyalties were being torn apart and he felt almost sorry for her, but he needed answers. Watching the scene unfold, he was having the greatest difficulty in keeping his mouth shut and letting her father do the talking. But that was the way he'd want it played if the boot was on the other foot and it was Adam in the hot seat.

'OK, look, maybe I should have told him not to go, but he was desperate to do something about Charlie . . .' Suzy put down her bag and reached for one of the coffees, took a sip and looked at Tony. 'He said he couldn't stand to watch his mum cry all the time, talking about her – about Charlie – like she was dead, and, you know, wait for other people to do things?'

Tony leant forward. 'And?'

'And he, um, he went there . . . to try and find her . . .'

Tony, mouth open, looked from Suzy to her father and back again. 'He did what?'

'Where did he go, Suzy?'

'Tokyo, Dad. He went to Tokyo . . .'

Walking down the street, back towards the capsule hotel, Adam saw a sign for a bar up on the fourth floor of a building; it had beer, it had cocktails and widescreen TV and it also had free Internet access. Adam stopped, remembering he'd promised Suzy that he would send her an email as soon as he'd arrived. Better do it now, rather than wait till tomorrow.

He looked up at the building, another one with signs advertising businesses on every floor – hairdressers, dentists, clubs, restaurants, beauticians – thinking how in London you'd think twice about going to some bound-to-be-scuzzy bar up off the street. He shrugged and started up the stairs, which, he was glad to note, did not smell like a toilet, figuring he'd probably have to buy a beer to get 'free' access to the Net. But what the hell, after scaring himself half to death in that back alley in Roppongi he thought he probably deserved a drink.

The place up on the fourth floor was called the Alfa, which apparently stood for All Life Feels Ace. Adam kind of almost knew what they meant. He walked into a small, dimly lit place with a bar running down one side, three computer terminals along the opposite wall, chairs and table in the centre and a tiny stage at the end. The place wasn't packed out, but it wasn't empty either, and the mostly suited crowd seemed to be enjoying the efforts of the guy up on the stage with the microphone. The widescreen TV was behind him and the lyrics to the song – bizarrely, 'Last Train to Clarksville' by The Monkees – came up as he sang, '. . . and I don't know if I'm ever coming home'. Which sounded to Adam way too much like the soundtrack to what he was doing.

He walked up to the bar, shaking off the feeling that he was in some weird movie, and waited until he was noticed by one of the barmen.

'Beer, please.'

'*Biru?*' Adam nodded hopefully. 'Asahi? Dry?'

'Sure, whatever . . .' Adam hoped he'd understood what the man had said and waited to see what he was getting.

Nodding his thanks when a bottle of beer was put on the bar in front of him, he paid, then pointed over his shoulder. 'Can I use the computer? Internet?'

'Intanetto? Mochiron!' The man did a kind of small bow, smiling broadly, and went off to serve another customer.

That's a yes, then, thought Adam, taking his beer and going over to one of the terminals. He sat down, moved the mouse to wake up the screen and logged on to Yahoo. One of the last things he'd done before leaving had been to check that his Yahoo account was still active. He'd never worked out how to access his home email address when he wasn't actually at home, had meant to get round to it but somehow'd never found the time. This other account was just a whole lot simpler.

I'm here, he typed, *and staying in a capsule. Going to start looking for Charlie tomorrow . . .* He stopped, wondering what else to say – he'd seen so much, but couldn't begin to describe any of it, and thought maybe that would have to wait. For now all he really had to do was let Suzy know he was OK . . . *I'm fine, will email soon. Love you too. Adam xxx*

He typed in Suzy's email address and sent the message off. He looked at his watch: 12:30. It was Thursday already.

17

Heaven and hermitage

One a.m. was obviously still early in Tokyo as hardly any of the capsules on Adam's floor were occupied. Loud snoring was coming from down near the door and he'd seen light from a TV flickering behind the drawn blind of another capsule as he'd climbed into his. Adam lay looking at the ceiling, all of an arm's reach away; tomorrow, absolute first thing, he had to find somewhere else to stay, because another night in this place – clean though it was – and he thought he might find himself suffering from claustrophobia.

If he wanted to get a really early start it would be a good idea to know where he was going when he got up, do the research now rather than simply lie around listening to the tiny night noises and waiting to go to sleep. Adam shuffled down the end of the capsule, raised the blind and climbed back down the two steps. He unlocked his locker, got out the Rough Guide and went back to what he couldn't help thinking of as 'his box'. As he was getting back in, a couple of men came stumbling out of the lift, both dressed in charcoal-grey suits, dark ties, white shirts, with thin black leather briefcases and as pissed as bishops. He wondered what kind of condition they'd be in come the morning.

Lying back down, he found the accommodation section in

the book, which had recommendations from under ¥3,000 to over ¥40,000. All he needed was something at the cheap end of the spectrum that he could at least stand up in. And a window would be nice. Not essential, but nice. Leafing through the pages, checking the price code (I – affordable, 9 – forget it), and then looking at where the hotels were on his map, he found there wasn't much choice anywhere and absolutely nothing in or even remotely near Roppongi. He should've been so lucky.

He narrowed things down to a hotel up in a place called Minowa, quite far out from the centre, but on one of the subway lines which ran through Roppongi. Adam began to fall asleep, hoping the place would have a vacancy, then remembered he hadn't set the alarm on his watch for an early start and had to turn the light back on to do it. He was gone the moment his head hit the pillow.

Keith Venner put the phone down and looked around the room for DC Thomson. He had a job for him. 'Anyone seen Eddy?'

'Fag break, sarge,' an unidentified voice coming from behind a computer screen over in the corner informed him.

'Bugger's only just had one . . .' Venner got up, stretched and was just about to go in search of his assistant when DC Thomson walked back into the room. 'Thought you were trying to give up the evil weed, Eddy.'

'It's not giving me up, sarge.'

'I had a call while you were out enjoying yourself.'

'Yeah?'

'Mr Grey.'

'Has he heard something?'

'You could say.' Venner sat back down at his desk. 'His son's gone missing now . . . guess where?'

'Well, if you know where he is, he can't be missing, sarge.'

'You'd think.'

'So,' Thomson shrugged, 'where is he?'

'Tokyo.'

'Get out!'

'As I live and breathe. Mr Grey tracked down the mystery girlfriend and apparently the boy took off yesterday.'

'Whereabouts is he in Tokyo?'

'That's what no one knows, but he's gone to look for his sister because, the girlfriend said, he didn't think anyone else was doing anything.'

'Silly sod . . . how was the dad?'

'He was angry and apologetic.' Venner neatened up some papers on his desk. 'His wife's a bit distraught, though – you can imagine, it's *both* kids now.'

'What're we going to do about this, then?'

'You're going over to the Greys' and picking up the kid's computer. The dad says he's tried looking for his emails but can't even turn the thing on. He's given us permission to have a go, so I want you to pick it up, bring it back and let that techy bloke – wassisname, Simons?' Thomson nodded. 'Let him have a go at it. OK?'

'Now?' Thomson looked at his watch.

'Yes, now . . . think of it as an extended fag break.' Thomson turned to pick up his jacket. 'And don't forget to take the paperwork for the parents to sign . . .'

'Sarge?'

'You're back . . . did you give the computer to Simons?'

'Yeah.'

'And?'

'And he can't open it up either. Says there's some quite heavy security on it that's going to take some breaking into.'

'Thought Simons was supposed to be a bit of a whiz-kid?'

'He is. He says it looks like the kind of protection hackers use to stop anyone doing to them what they do to other people. He says he can get past it, but it'll take longer than he expected. D'you think this Adam kid's a hacker, sarge?'

'No idea, I'll call the dad and ask – but don't hold your breath, they seem to know very little about what their son gets up to.' Venner picked up the phone. 'Go back and see how Simons is doing, I'll come down in a minute . . .'

Eddy Thomson looked up as the door to the room he and Simons were in opened and Keith Venner came in.

'Nothing doing so far, sarge.'

Simons sat back, frowning. 'What did the boy's dad say?'

The DS walked round the table to look at the screen Adam Grey's computer had been plugged into; it looked like a really ancient computer, a black screen with small typewriter writing and lots of arrows and stuff. 'He using something really old?'

Simons shook his head as he leant forward, typed a few keystrokes and hit return. 'No, this is DOS, what runs under all the flash stuff. Did you get anything that might help here?'

'Oh, right. Yeah, Tony Grey, the dad, says as far as he knows Adam was a gamer, not a hacker – played a lot online.'

'Well, *someone* did a number on this machine.'

Venner looked at the piece of paper in his hand. 'The dad gave me some stuff here – girlfriend's name: Suzy Barrett;

dog: Badger; his birthday: 25/7/1987; star sign: Leo . . . are we clutching at straws here?'

'Dunno . . . got anything else?' Simons began writing stuff down on a pad.

'Mother: Sarah; father: Anthony, or Tony; sister: Charlie or Charlotte; favourite musician: Jimi Hendrix; favourite food: chilli; supports Tottenham – can't be all bad – and used to be called Adders by his mates, but that was way back in junior school . . .'

Simons scribbled something on his pad. 'How old's the dog?'

Thomson snorted and Venner made a puzzled face. 'How the hell should I know – why?'

'Nothing . . .' Simons stopped writing and looked at the scribbled notes he'd made on a pad next to the keyboard. 'All I need is a word, a key . . .' He picked up his biro and began scribbling again, then typed something into the computer. The screen cleared and Thomson and Venner found themselves looking at a window asking them to input their password.

'Have you got something, Simons?' Venner pulled up a chair and sat down.

'I've got an idea . . .' He typed six different characters, small black dots appearing in the box in the middle of the window, then slowly put his finger on the return key and pressed it. 'Light a candle, guv . . .'

The screen blanked and cleared to reveal a background picture of Jimi Hendrix, going full throttle on some stage. Two columns of Windows icons ran down the left-hand side of the screen and when Simons moved the mouse the cursor tracked across it.

Simons sat back smiling. 'We're in!'

'How did you do it? Was it the girlfriend?' Venner looked at the notes Simons had made.

'A girlfriend's a girlfriend, guv, but a dog is for life, right?'

'So?'

'So I figured it was gonna be Badger, not Suzy or anything else – but it wouldn't be *that* simple.' Simons picked up the pad, turned over to a fresh page and wrote something. 'You know those stupid personalised number plates, the ones where they haven't quite got the right letters and use numbers for vowels?'

Thomson and Venner both nodded and Simons turned the pad round and held it up so they could see what he'd written.

B4DG3R

'I was lucky, it would've taken a hell of a lot longer without that. Where to now, guv?'

'Log on to his email account and see what's been going on there and print everything out. Eddy, let's go and see if anything's come in from Interpol. And then I'll buy you a beer.'

'OK, sarge.' Thomson pushed himself off the wall he'd been leaning on to follow his boss. 'Why d'you think he's got all this security on his computer, Simons?'

'Probably because he could. I reckon he knows someone who *is* a hacker and got him to do it. I'll give the hard drive a good going over, but . . .' he glanced at the PC tower on the desk to his left, '. . . I'll be honest, this doesn't look like your typical piece of hacker kit. Straight out the box from PCWorld, this is.'

Adam's watch alarm went off at 7:00 a.m. and he spent

what seemed like ages trying to find it before remembering it was on his wrist. He got out of his capsule as quietly as he could, not wanting to wake anyone else, and saw that well over half of the blinds were drawn. Obviously a lot of late nights last night.

Getting his travel bag out of his locker he went to the bathroom and by 7:45 he was standing out on the early morning street. He'd bought a chocolate bar and a soft drink from the vending machines in the hotel foyer and was having 'breakfast' as he walked. Looking to his right before he crossed the road to go to the Asakusa subway station, he saw a weird object on the other side of the bridge.

As he might not be coming back this way, Adam waited for a gap in the traffic and crossed diagonally to take a closer look at what appeared to be a massive gold turd that had been ever-so-carefully laid on top of a highly polished black stone plinth. It didn't look like a building, no windows he could see. Could it be a piece of sculpture? If a cow cut in half and put in embalming fluid was art, then why not a gold turd? Maybe it was a comment – *all art is crap!* – you never knew. Whatever it was, it was worth a picture, which he would've taken if he'd remembered to bring his camera with him. Which he hadn't. He'd noticed the night before that a lot of places sold disposable cameras, and turning to walk back towards the station he made a mental note to buy one as soon as he saw some on sale.

'Guv?' Simons poked his head round the door and saw DS Venner and DC Thomson looking like they were about to make an exit at the end of their shift; all packed and ready to go.

Venner looked up. 'Yeah?'

'Found something you might want to see before you go, guv.'

'You printed it out?'

Simons waved a sheet of paper. 'Ta-dah!'

'Let's have a look.' Venner waved Simons into the room and reached out for the print-out.

'What's it say?' Thomson walked behind his boss to read over his shoulder.

Venner read the two lines of type. *Hi! sorry i've not been in touch. bin frantic, lots to tell, will mail soon. Luv C,'* and sat back, looking up at Simons. 'Why the fuss about this particular email?'

'Look at the date, guv.'

'Bloody hell!'

'What, sarge?' Thomson leant over to take a closer look.

'It's yesterday, that's what, Eddy.'

'And it doesn't sound like someone who's been kidnapped, does it, guv?'

'Not a lot.'

Thomson stood up, shaking his head. 'All a fuss over nothing, then, right? Are you gonna call the parents and tell 'em?'

'Hold on, Ed.' Venner waved a 'calm down' hand at his DC. 'How do we know this email actually came from the girl? The brother's address could've been forced out of her and anyone could've sent it. I mean there's definitely something going on, what with the other girl, Alice . . .' Venner snapped his fingers, trying to remember Alice's surname.

'Reardon, is it, boss?'

'Right, Ed, Alice Reardon. What is it with her going missing too?' Venner sat back in his chair and scratched his head. 'No, the email doesn't mean a thing, it's just virtual. There needs to be *actual* contact.'

'Are you not telling Mr and Mrs Grey, then?'

'Don't think so, not immediately, not until Simons here has had a go at finding out exactly where this email was sent from.' Venner looked up at Simons. 'You can do that, can't you?'

'I can have a go, guv.' Simons looked at his watch. 'I probably won't get very far tonight as I'll need some help from the service provider, and you might have to get some-one upstairs to do a bit of asking for me . . . but I'll get started.'

As he turned to leave the room, Thomson moved round from behind his boss's desk. 'Hang on a sec – shouldn't we reply?'

Venner frowned. 'What?'

'If the brother had actually got the message, he'd've replied, right? Sent a message straight back?' Thomson looked from his boss to Simons and back. 'So shouldn't we send a reply back for him and see what happens?'

'Good thinking, Eddy – go with Simons and check out how he's replied to her in the past and rough out a mes-sage and then I'll tell the parents we're doing it.'

'I thought –'

'Changed my mind – DS's prerogative. While you're doing that I'll see if I can get something moving upstairs. Who's she got her email account with, Simons?'

'Yahoo, guv.'

Venner reached for the phone, glancing at a list of exten-sions taped to the desk. 'Thanks . . . I'll be along in a minute.' Before he could dial the number his phone rang. 'DS Venner . . . Oh, hello, Mr Grey . . . right, Suzy, the girlfriend . . . an email from Adam . . . OK, thanks for letting me know, and if you could ask her father to let us have a print-out that would be a great help . . . right . . . no, nothing new . . . as soon as I know anything I'll let you know, Mr Grey. Right, thanks . . . Goodnight.'

Venner put the phone down, wondering if he should've told Tony Grey right then about the email from his daughter. Getting people's hopes up and then having to let them down was, in his opinion, worse than keeping them in the dark until you were sure of what you were talking about.

18

In travelling, a wonder resort

It was only five stops, with one change, to Minowa station, and then, said the guidebook, the hotel was a ten-minute walk. Adam had come out at ground level opposite a McDonald's and immediately caught a whiff of burgers, fries and ketchup. A chocolate bar was not a breakfast, a small but insistent voice in his head kept on saying, and he had to admit he did still feel hungry. He was going to have to do a lot of walking today, and in the end, why not? Being both quick and cheap it ticked at least two of his boxes right now.

Adam ordered an orange juice to go with his meal, to give it at least a semblance of being healthy, and was back out on the street in no time flat. He had no idea what this hotel was going to be like, but if cheap hotels in London were anything to go by – and this place was supposedly even less expensive than the capsule hotel he'd just stayed in – then he was preparing himself for the worst. Some of the B&B hotels you saw clustered round the mainline stations in London looked like you wouldn't even put your dog there for the night.

In his mind's eye he saw an image of Badger, the one member of the household he could always guarantee would be glad to see him, whatever time of day or night it was. Not something he could ever say about the rest of his family. Adam had to stop himself thinking like this, as the train of thought was taking him places he did not want to go, getting him to think about things he'd prefer to keep wrapped up. Like his parents, what he'd done coming here, that he had less than a bat's chance in hell of ever finding Charlie. And what he would feel like if anything final happened to Grangie while he was away. Negative, negative, negative.

Look on the bright side, he told himself. It wasn't raining, the sun was shining, and this was good because he wasn't exactly going to be spending a lot of time relaxing in his room. He looked round for some kind of signpost to give him a clue as to where he was, but it appeared that they weren't big on street names in Tokyo, even in Japanese. This was not going to be a ten-minute walk like the book had said; make that half an hour, easy, maybe more if he really went off course, as he searched in vain for some clue as to which way he should be going.

He realised later he must've looked like the archetypal Lost Tourist, standing on a corner with luggage, wearing a small backpack and a puzzled expression and peering at a map. He was just wondering about going into a shop and seeing how he got on asking for directions, when a man wearing a peaked cap, some kind of uniform and pulling a cart stopped next to him and smiled, nodding. Adam nodded back.

He held up his map. 'New Economy Hotel?'

'Ah!' The man – Adam now realised he was a postman – grinned even more. *'Chikai!'* Adam watched as he pointed down the road to his right, held up three fingers and indicated he should go left. *'Shingo . . .'* he said, looking back

118

up the road and pointing at the traffic lights. *'Shingo,'* he repeated, and made the 'go left' sign again.

OK, Adam thought, sounds like three roads down and go left by some traffic lights; he repeated the mimed instructions, the postman nodding as he did so and then holding up his hand, 'stop', making the 'go left' again.

'Meiji-dori, mittsume no shingo.' The postman held up three fingers again and made a 'go right' sign and said something Adam couldn't make head nor tail of.

'Turn left, go past three traffic lights and then take a right . . . is that where the New Economy is?'

'Hai! Hoteru – Economy!'

'Thanks, thanks very much.' Adam did a small bow, like he'd seen people doing, and held out his hand.

The postman shook it, smiling, and bowed himself. *'Sayonara!'*

'Sayonara, mate . . .'

Adam could see the third set of traffic lights just up ahead, and beyond them the right turn that should, if he'd understood the postman's instructions correctly, be the road that the New Economy Hotel was on. He checked his watch and saw it was 9:30 – he'd been walking for almost ten minutes. He quickened his pace, wanting to see if he really was where he should be or if he was going to have to go through the whole map-and-mime process again. He wanted to get the hotel thing out of the way as quickly as possible so he could get on with trying to find the Bar Belle and Alice.

A couple of minutes later he was at the corner and, on the second block down the street, he thought he could see a black and white sign on a red brick building with a lot of bicycles outside it on the pavement; budget hotel, budget transport.

It was 10:15 and Adam was on his way back to Minowa station. He didn't have a room yet as the hotel was fully booked, but he was fairly sure the guy at the reception, who'd really tried very hard with his English, had said that someone was leaving today. He'd managed to make Adam understand he should leave a deposit and had then let him leave his backpack, telling him to call back after midday. 'Something for you, no probrem!' he'd said, smiling. Well, Adam bloody well hoped so.

Walking down the street, the sun hot on the back of his neck, the feeling of almost total insecurity – nowhere to stay, no one to talk to, no real idea whether he was doing the right thing – was building knots of tension in his shoulders and his stomach. Adam stopped walking and stood for a moment, letting the rest of Tokyo carry on while he tried to get a grip, come to terms with where he was, the situation he was in. The situation *he'd* put himself in. No one else around to blame for anything, no one else around to look to for reassurance that he wasn't being a complete arse. He was in one of the biggest, busiest cities in the whole world, and he might as well be in the middle of the Sahara for all the help he'd got available to him.

Out of the corner of one eye he saw a shiny, pearlescent black bird fly down off the roof of a nearby building and land untidily in the gutter a few feet away from him. It looked like a crow, a raven, a rook or something like that. Big, with a massive beak and a swaggering, cocksure walk like it owned the place, the bird stopped for a moment before pecking at something in the dust . . . Adam saw it was the remains of a very dead pigeon. Was that cannibalism, one bird eating another bird? Did birds do that? The crow or raven or whatever it was looked up at him, turning its polished head sideways, a glittering eye staring up at him – like, what's your problem, and who the hell are you anyway? Above, on the rooftops, Adam could hear other birds cawing and realised he'd been hearing the sound all morning, that Tokyo had crows the way London had pigeons. He turned away, somehow not wanting to be the subject of the bird's disdainful glance, not wanting to see the go-home-loser look on its face.

A soft fluttering noise, like someone waving a silk scarf, made Adam look back. The crow, which'd obviously found there was nothing left worth bothering with on the feathered carcass in the gutter, was going back up where it'd come from. The bird cawed loudly as it took off, dust rising in a faint cloud, then circled and lazily flapped its way up to a balcony where it landed, raised its tail and crapped. Nice.

Adam started walking again; he'd picked up a small, pocket-sized subway map at the hotel, as well as the information that he should buy something called a Passnet card. For the equivalent of about a fiver, he'd be able to use any of the lines run by the three different train companies who operated the Tokyo subway system. This sounded a hell of a lot easier than trying to negotiate the ticket machines every time he wanted to take a ride.

Roppongi was, like any night-time place, a very pale shadow in broad daylight, bleached of all its gaudy colours. Quieter, stripped of their glamour and their dark energy, the streets had the air of a circus waking up the morning after a performance, all the props still in place but the performers either asleep or without make-up and no longer recognisable.

What had been a seamless combination of neon mayhem playing against a matt-black sky was, by day, an untidy, looping mess of wiring, strung from tall poles, lacing down the streets, criss-crossing the roads, feeding the buildings with power and light and connections. What would be hidden underground back home was out on show here, and looked like it had been put up in a hurry by someone who hadn't got a plan, worked by rule of thumb and had done everything totally piecemeal – strangely Third World electrics in this electronic city.

Adam figured that a lot of the bars probably wouldn't be open yet, but he felt safer walking round back streets now than he'd done the night before. All he had to do was find the Bar Belle and then come back when it was open. *All* he had to do. He shook his head; as if it was going to be that easy. Standing at the crossroads, with the flyover running right and left, he decided to get logical. Using the small map at the back of the guidebook he mentally divided the area up into sections, like roughly quartering a square, planning to walk as many of the streets in each 'section' as he could.

Somewhere round here, probably not far from where he was, there had to be a street or an alleyway where he'd find the Bar Belle. Charlie had only ever mentioned the place a couple of times, but she had said it was in Roppongi and he was going to find it or wear out his shoes trying.

As he began his search, Adam became more and more aware of how different this part of Tokyo was to the few other bits he'd seen. He was used to the way the Japanese raided English for words that looked cool, felt right but did not make any kind of sense – like what the hell did the word Walkman actually mean, right? But here in Roppongi there were many more words in English, there were 'Irish' pubs ('Roast beef lunch on Sundays!') and even a Jazz Café London, and far more Westerners on the street – *gaijin*, as the guidebook's glossary said foreigners were called, like him. Some were obviously tourists, but the groups of tall, skinny, bleach-blonde girls, all crop-tops, pierced navels, high heels and speaking what sounded like some ex-Soviet bloc language as they traipsed past him, they were different. These people weren't hanging out, they were waiting, biding time.

Adam was fairly sure they were bar girls and hostesses who might well know where the Bar Belle was, but they didn't look very approachable and exuded an aura of you-lookin-at-me? that was way more fuck off than friendly. He decided to do what he could on his own before asking for help, and carried on his way.

It was still only ten thirty and a lot of the shops at street level hadn't yet opened – shutters locked down tight, lights out – but Adam's problem was that none of the bars were actually at street level, they were either in basements or somewhere up dark, narrow stairways on one of the upper floors, where a lot of business seemed to be done off ground level.

In London it was rare for a shop not to have a street-level frontage, and you'd only ever go upstairs once you'd checked a place out first. Dodgy travel agencies and 'Schools of English' were the only places he'd seen with signs in doorways, on the look-out to attract punters to go up dingy staircases. After an hour he'd done the first of his 'sections', the north-east one on his map, and had found nothing. There were plenty of bars, restaurants and clubs, but none of them were the Bar Belle.

With one down and three more 'sections' to go, Adam crossed the busy street at a set of lights, going under the expressway to the other side. To his right he could see the massive curved high-rise tower at the centre of what the book told him was called Roppongi Hills, a kind of up-market shopping mall with gardens and restaurants, cinemas and museums. Not hostess bars. He turned left and was about to take the first side street when he saw a bank of vending machines with a huge selection of cold drinks on sale, none of which looked at all familiar. But he was hot and he was thirsty, and, while the thought of drinking something called Pocari Sweat didn't light up his life, it was obviously extremely popular as he'd seen quite a few Japanese youth knocking it back.

In for a penny, in for ¥110, he thought, dropping a couple of coins in the slot. As the can dropped into the collection bay it occurred to Adam that they'd probably got the word wrong and had meant to call it Pocari Sweet.

19

The spirited luxury for nice couples

'Scuse me?'

Adam poked his head round the half-open door at the bottom of a stairwell that led into somewhere called, appropriately enough, The Pit. It was the first bar he'd come across that appeared to be open. The place's sound system was up and running, and over a loud, wailing saxophone someone was singing, 'Old England is dying, his clothes a dirty shade of blue and ancient shoes worn through . . .' Adam thought that young England could well be in the same state after today, the shoe bit anyway.

The girl behind the small bar looked up and then over her blue-lensed sunglasses at him. 'Not open, mate.' Australian, maybe a Kiwi. She glanced at her watch. 'Come back at five o'clock.'

Adam stayed where he was. 'I don't want a drink, just want to ask a question – can I come in for a minute?'

'Yeah, sure.' The girl picked up a lit cigarette from a nearby ashtray, took a drag and went on wiping the bar down with a grey cloth. 'What d'you want to know?'

'You heard of a place called the Bar Belle?'

'Yeah, why?'

'I'm trying to find it.'

'It's no great shakes, mate, there's better places to go looking for.' The girl eyed him up and down. 'I mean, you don't look like the typical hostess bar clientele.'

'It's actually someone who works there I'm after.' Adam walked over to the bar and took out the photo of Charlie and Alice he'd brought with him. He showed it to the girl. 'D'you know either of them?'

The girl reached over, took the print and gave it a cursory glance. 'Can't say I do.' She handed it back.

'The one with the blonde hair? That's my sister.' Adam tucked the picture back in the Rough Guide.

'That right . . .'

'She was working at the Bar Belle, but she's missing, and I'm trying to find her. Alice, the other one, was working there too and I need to talk to her.'

'Yeah? Well the Belle's off behind the Higashi-dori, past Gaspanic? It's up towards Ark Hills, in the point of the triangle the two expressways make.' The girl ran a tap and began rinsing her cloth. 'Know where I mean?'

'Not really, would you mind showing me on the map?'

The girl stubbed out her cigarette, took the map Adam handed her and opened it up. 'We're here,' she jabbed the map with a fingernail in dire need of repainting, 'that's the Higashi-dori and there's the two expressways. The Belle's in there, or it was the last time I was over that way . . . these places open and close like a fish's mouth.'

Adam took the map back. 'Thanks . . . I'll um, I'll let you get on.'

'No problem, I hope you find her, your sister and her friend.'

'Me too . . .'

The girl stopped and looked at him, frowning slightly. 'When you said missing did you mean just not around, or like really *missing*?'

'Alice said she saw her walking out of the place with some Japanese guy about ten days ago, and that's the last she's seen of her. That kind of missing.'

'Jeez.' The girl shook her head. 'Sorry to hear that . . . hope you find her, mate.'

'Thanks . . .'

It was well after midday when Adam stopped on the edge of the pavement and looked across the Higashi-dori. To his right, way down the road, he could see this big, red and white, more modern version of the Eiffel Tower dominating the skyline, and wondered if you could go up it and what the view of Tokyo would be like from there. Maybe, once he'd found Charlie, they could see a couple of the sights before they went home.

Maybe . . . but maybe he'd never find Charlie. Alive, anyway.

She could be dead. He knew that was a possibility, although it was one he could choose to ignore, even though he knew that wouldn't make it go away, wouldn't make it an *im*possibility. Just thinking these things made him feel physically sick, like throwing up right there. Except there was nothing in his stomach and, along with this awful nausea, there was a completely contradictory gnawing hunger.

Shaking off the depressing sense of helplessness, Adam waited for a gap in the traffic and crossed the road. If this part of Roppongi was anything like the other bits he'd trawled through this morning, he'd find some small, cheap restaurant off the main drag with a window display of plastic food and get himself some lunch. Then, after he'd eaten, he'd search out and find the Bar Belle – and the later he left it the more likely it was the place would be open. He walked down the street, towards where the girl in The Pit had said this place called Gaspanic was located, and a few minutes later he saw it, off to his left down a small side street.

It was amazing. Back home the pictures stuck in the window of any fast food outlet you cared to choose – the massive, metre-wide food porno, glossy, pumped-up burgers with artistically arranged strips of bacon and slices of pickle and tomato in pillowy sesame buns – looked totally nothing like the sad thing some no-star server handed over in a polystyrene box. So not what you got here in Japan. OK, so his lunch hadn't cost him 99p, but what you saw in the window was *exactly* like what you got on your plate. And it also tasted great.

He felt more like vegging out after his meal than going back to pounding the pavements, but he was on a mission and he couldn't allow himself to relax until later. He could do that *after* he'd found the Bar Belle. Alice could be there right now. She might know something more about where Charlie was. You never knew, something good could happen.

It occurred to Adam that he should contact Suzy and see if anything good *had* happened already and he didn't know about it. Then again, should he contact the police here in Tokyo, try and find out what they knew? As he threaded his way through the maze of narrow streets Adam found it difficult to concentrate on looking for some sign of the Bar

Belle at the same time as trying to work out what he should do. What would happen if he went to the police? How would they react to the younger brother of a missing English girl turning up unannounced? Might be a very bad idea . . . best try to do what he could on his own.

Adam looked at the time. Nearly two o'clock. Two o'clock! His useless damn memory – he hadn't rung the hotel to check whether they had a room for him tonight! Finding a payphone was going to have to take temporary priority over finding the bar. He remembered seeing a bank of phones in Roppongi station near the ticket machines and cursed himself, as he turned to go back there, for not remembering when he was nearer.

Pushing in the phone card he'd bought from a vending machine, wondering if there was anything you couldn't buy out of a slot machine in this city, Adam punched in the number of the New Economy Hotel and listened to the alien ring tone, waiting for the call to be picked up.

Click. 'New Economy?' A girl's voice.

'Oh, hi . . . d'you speak English?'

'Yes, littre.'

'I came this morning, to book a room?'

'Room, yes.'

'But there wasn't one ready.'

'Room not ready?'

'Not ready this morning. The man said to call back after midday, after 12 o'clock.'

'Name?'

'The man? I dunno . . . he didn't say . . .'

'*You* name, prease.'

'Sorry – Adam, Adam Grey . . . I wrote it down, and I left

my backpack as well.'

'Sure, sure, I got it, Mister Grey – you want room?'

'There's a room?'

'Sure, sure, you want?'

'*Yes!*' Adam pulled a punch, grinning like a mad man. 'Result!'

'Excuse me?'

'Yes please, I'd like the room – from tonight, OK?'

'How long for, Mister Grey?'

That stopped Adam in his tracks. How long should he book for? A week? Just a couple of days, and see how it goes? He hadn't thought this bit through at all.

'You there, Mister Grey?'

'Yeah, right, sorry . . . um . . .' think, think, '. . . seven days? Can I have the room for a week?'

'Sure, sure, no probrem, Mister Grey, see you tonight.'

'Thanks . . . yeah, see you tonight.'

As Adam put the phone down he felt a weight lift off his shoulders. One less thing to worry about. Taking his phone card he went back up to street level and set off on his search again.

It was hot, the sun beating down from a cloudless, pale blue sky, and he got his sunglasses out of his backpack. Walking down the Higashi-dori, back towards where he'd had his lunch, he spotted what looked like a Japanese version of a Poundstretcher, a cheap-and-cheerful, pile 'em high place that was bound to have throwaway cameras. He waited for a gap in the traffic and crossed over.

There was a big ¥100 sign hanging above the open frontage and signs all over the place in Japanese that Adam figured must mean things like *BARGAIN!* and *GIVE-AWAY*

PRICES! Inside the shop was jammed, literally floor to ceiling, with deodorants, torches, crockery, shampoos, plastic kitchen equipment, gaudy knick-knacks, underwear, socks, gadgets, and everything in no specific order or obvious logic that he could work out. He finally found a dumpbin of disposable cameras. Sorted.

Having paid, he was back across the street and walking past the Gaspanic when he saw a sign saying every Thursday, all drinks, all night, were ¥400 and admission was free. Two quid. Not bad, maybe he'd swing by later. As he was about to plunge back into the web of side streets a couple of girls walked by handing out leaflets, and a colour A5 flyer was shoved into his hand, printed on just one side. He found himself staring at the weirdest illustration of a pair of feet with red toes, eyes staring back at him from underneath the second and third toes and the rest of each foot covered in strange drawings. On closer inspection the drawings were of things like a heart, kidneys, a liver and intestines, and tiny English type under Japanese characters told him that other coloured areas denoted things like the nose, knee and buttock. Adam thought it might be for an acupuncture or acupressure clinic. His mum had had acupressure on her feet once, for a bad back, and he remembered his dad taking the piss out of the whole thing. He couldn't remember if it had worked or not.

Still reading the annotations on the flyer, Adam turned off the sunlit street he was on and went into a shaded, narrow side road, looking up for a moment to see if this was somewhere he recognised and had already checked out before he went to call the hotel. The change from bright sunlight to deep shadow, combined with the sunglasses, meant his eyes momentarily turned everything he looked at into not much more than dark shapes. Adam pushed the plastic frames up on to his forehead to see better. And there she was.

Alice.

He stopped walking. It was her, he was sure of it. Up ahead, some twenty, thirty metres away, the girl who looked exactly like Alice also stopped, and for the longest couple of seconds they stared at each other. She was at the back of a small crowd of Japanese people, standing half a head taller than them, and she looked shocked, eyes wide, mouth slightly open, then a frown. Before Adam had a chance to call or wave or anything, the girl – it was Alice, absolutely, completely no doubt about it – turned and ran away.

20

Bitter and stupid

'*ALICE!*'

Rooted to the spot, Adam yelled at the top of his voice at the retreating back of his sister's best friend . . . what the hell was happening? Why was she running away when surely she should be pleased to see him? Surely . . .

He saw the faces of the people walking towards him – staring, like, what was this *gaijin* doing? – and then Alice had disappeared round a corner. The statue spell was broken. Adam pulled his sunglasses back down and started to run, pushing his way through the knot of pedestrians, not even bothering to apologise, too focused to care about being polite.

Alice had a good head start on him, and by the time he'd got past all the people and reached the turn she'd taken, she was nowhere to be seen. There were people about, but he knew he'd waste too much time trying to pantomime, '*Have you seen an English girl with straight black hair running this way?*', so he didn't and carried on running himself.

First turning, nothing, no sign; next a crossroads – left, nothing – right . . . yes! There she was, he could see her down the end of the narrow road, running and glancing over her shoulder, with black hair swinging. It had to be

Alice. Adam took off like a rocket and went as if he was going for gold, his mind on one thing only: catching Alice and finding out why she'd run. His feet pounded on the asphalt, his arms pumped and he streaked past piles of beer crates filled with empties, past lighted vending machines and darkened entrances to tiny restaurants and bars and clubs, past metal poles with intense nests of electrical wiring and under what looked like junction boxes hung across the street only a couple of metres above his head. All the time all his concentration centred on keeping Alice in sight and shortening the distance between them.

He was catching her up fast, closing the gap and feeling more certain with every blurring pace that he was seconds away from winning this race. Ahead he saw that the road they were on led directly into what looked like a main street and then Alice had reached the junction, turned a sharp right and was gone again. Adam pushed himself forward, skidding to a halt and grabbing on to a post to stop himself from blundering into the passing foot traffic. He stared down the street. Alice was nowhere.

Standing, panting for breath, Adam took off his sunglasses and stared the way Alice had run. The pavement was crowded with hundreds, make that thousands of people, all with straight black hair, walking towards him and away from him. It was like one of those truly frustrating dreams where every move you make is thwarted and the thing you want more than anything else in the world is always tantalisingly out of reach, never in your grasp. But this was real; he could smell the traffic fumes, hear the cawing of the crows, feel the heat of the city. He was not going to wake from this and find everything was just fine with his world.

Alice had been there, only metres away, and now she'd disappeared, along with any chances he might have had of finding out who had taken Charlie and where she might be. If Alice had run away the moment she'd seen him, Adam had a fair idea it wasn't likely she would be hanging round the Bar Belle, waiting for him, when he eventually found it.

He swore; a loud, primal, vicious, nasty stream of verbal bile. An old woman, dressed in a traditional kimono, grey hair pulled back into a neat bun, looked at him, a shocked expression on her face. This time, before he went off down the street in the vain hope of seeing Alice again, he apologised.

Before he'd gone more than a hundred metres Adam knew it was hopeless. He was never going to find her now; if she didn't want to see him there were any number of side streets she could have taken to get away, even crossing the road and going off who knew where. Chasing Alice was going to be a complete waste of time, but she'd been so close it was hard to give up and walk away.

He stopped at the edge of the pavement, cars, scooters, buses, bicycles streaming past him on his left, a constant flow of people to his right. Everything around him moving, him with nowhere to go. He supposed the only thing he could do now was get back to trying to find the Bar Belle, seeing if anyone there knew anything about Charlie, or why Alice didn't want to see him. He really should make a move . . .

Across the pavement he noticed a man pushing up the shutters of a shop to reveal the windows: windows totally full of cages, each about the size of big microwave, each with a tiny kitten or a puppy in it. Adam walked over to have a look, fascinated; you never saw pets shops in

England any more, at least he couldn't remember the last time he'd seen one. A small, golden-coloured dachshund, standing in a cage at his eye level, looked right at him through the glass, tail wagging, the epitome of cute. If it could talk, thought Adam, it would be saying 'Buy *me*!'. Feeling mildly depressed, standing there in front of a wall of boxed creatures, Adam turned and walked away. Everyone was selling something in this world, even a puppy. He didn't look back.

Sometimes, thought Adam, because that's the way things were, after searching like your life depended on it, you found stuff when you weren't really looking, had given up all hope and set your mind elsewhere. It was coming up to six o'clock and Adam was making his way towards the Gaspanic and happy hour. The last thing he felt was happy, but a drink surrounded by people who weren't completely pissed off could well change his mood.

He turned a corner into a street he thought would take him back in the right direction, a street he hadn't been down before, and there it was. The Bar Belle. Or at least a black plastic sign, stuck out from a wall above a door, with red neon letters that spelt out the name. The sign was on, which should, if there was any kind of justice, mean the place was open. Adam almost ran to the entrance.

3F was what it said on the sign, which he had now figured out meant the third floor, but, here in Tokyo, the first floor was at street level. He walked up two flights of dimly lit stairs and found himself on a small landing looking through a doorway. It was open. He nodded to himself, seeing this as a good omen. The entrance led into a room that, like the sign downstairs, was painted black and lit by red light bulbs. He took a deep breath and walked in.

It was early, for a club, and the place looked empty, although it was hard to tell if there was anyone lurking in the deeper, air-conditioned shadows. Adam looked to his right, at the pool of white light where the bar was; no one there either. He walked over, pulled out a black vinyl upholstered stool and sat down with his back to the bar. Somebody was sure to turn up sooner or later, and while he waited he tried to imagine Charlie and Alice here . . . working. God, his dad would go nuts if he saw the place, because it was hard *not* to think what could go on in the booths lining both the walls.

'You been here long?'

A female voice, American accent, broke the silence, and as Adam jerked his head round to see who was talking he could hear the bones and muscle in his so-tense neck click and crack as they twisted. Behind him a Japanese woman stood at the bar; she was small, her black hair streaked with shiny platinum blonde, with multiple ear piercings and a monochrome tattoo of a roaring lion's head covering most of her right shoulder. Her lipstick was so dark it almost looked black, her skin was white like snow and she was wearing a skin-tight, sleeveless black T-shirt that made it very obvious she wasn't wearing a bra.

'No . . . no, not long . . .' Adam, glancing down at the woman's suddenly prominent nipples, could feel himself blushing and looked back up again.

The woman looked right at him and smiled, her lips slightly parted, and Adam was sure he could see a pair of arrow-sharp teeth. 'What can I get you?'

'Ah . . .' the teeth really were pointed, ' . . . a beer? Please . . .'

'You from UK?'

'Yeah . . . London.' Adam thought the woman looked like she'd come straight off the set of a horror flick. 'You?'

'Me? I'm from LA, originally, got here by way of Anchorage, Sydney, Auckland, Manila and a good few less well-known and all together best forgotten places in between.' She turned and got a bottle from one of the glass-fronted fridges behind her, chunked it open and put it in front of him. 'Glass?'

Adam shook his head, picked the bottle up and took a pull. The beer was so cold he thought his teeth would break, and he could feel it going all the way to his stomach, an icy hand moving down his chest.

'Have I met you before?'

Adam shook his head. 'No, I'm sure I'd remember . . . why?'

'You look familiar.'

'My sister worked here.'

'She did? Who was that, then?'

'Charlie Grey.'

Pause. Silence. Tight smile.

'You don't say.'

'She's gone missing.'

'Tell me about it.' The woman frowned. 'We had the police all over us like a rash, *not* good for business, and then Alice took off like a rabbit. Left me two girls down, which was a shitter.'

'Is this your place?'

'Mine?' The woman laughed. 'I'm just the mama-san around here, look after the girls, make sure everyone understands the rules . . .' She stopped and looked sideways at Adam. 'Why're *you* here?'

'I'm trying to find Charlie.'

'You come over with your parents?'

Truth or lie? Did it matter? 'I'm on my own.'

'That right?' Raised eyebrow, looking him up and down. 'Where you staying?'

'Some place called the New Economy?'

'And you've come here . . .' the woman indicated, with her chin, over Adam's shoulder at the club behind him, '. . . to check out if someone here might know where she could be and forgot to tell the cops?'

There was an edge to the woman's voice, like she thought Adam was accusing her of something. 'Look, all we've heard direct is what Alice said when she called and told my parents Charlie'd gone missing –'

'That she'd seen her walk out of here with a customer?' the woman butted in. 'Bullshit! Never happened!'

'What?'

'Like I said, there are rules; this isn't a whore house, no walking off the premises with clients – they want to meet later, do whatever *for* whatever, that's fine by me. But your sister did *not* leave here with a customer, OK? I told the cops that, and if that little bitch Alice had still been here when they arrived I'd've made her tell them the exact same thing, too.'

'When did she go?' Adam couldn't quite believe what he was hearing, but then he'd never believed Charlie would be so stupid as to get mixed up in something she couldn't handle.

'Alice? She went that same weekend Charlie's supposed to've "disappeared".' The woman made inverted commas with her fingers. 'Except Charlie had been gone a couple of days already; I hadn't seen the two girls together for some time and I've not seen Alice since she took her money that Saturday night. Like I told the cops.'

'I saw Alice today.'

'Where?'

'Round here, somewhere . . . she ran away the moment she saw me.'

'Alice, round here? You sure?'

Adam shrugged. 'Looked like her.'

'She'd've pissed her pants if she'd seen me . . .'

21

Flavorous and delicious communication

The woman, this goth/vampire bar manager-cum-Head Girl who said she was called Miki, hadn't got a lot of other information to give Adam; also, as they talked, customers began arriving in ones and twos and as they did so girls started appearing from the back of the club to join them at their chosen table or booth.

The girls, all of them European, most of them blonde like Charlie, were in some kind of cliché costume: nurse, schoolgirl, punk geisha – a lot of make-up, not a huge amount of clothes. Adam found himself wondering what Alice and Charlie had dressed up as and then realised he really did not want to know that kind of detail. It was becoming obvious, too, that Miki felt she'd done her bit and it was time for him to leave the premises. He was taking up space better used by a paying customer.

'What d'you think happened to Charlie if she didn't go off with a customer?' Adam got off the stool and put his empty bottle on the bar.

'I never said she didn't go off with a customer.' Miki took the bottle. 'I just said she didn't leave *here* with one. Big difference.'

'Did you ever meet Alice's boyfriend?'

'Steve? Yeah, he'd come by most nights, to pick 'em up. Why?'

'You've not seen him since either?'

'Look, guy, they all three of them dropped off the radar at around the same time. For all I know they just decided to go on their merry way and forgot to tell anyone. Working here is not what you call a career move, know what I mean?'

'So what's Alice still doing round here?'

'I think you've made the tragic error of mistaking me for someone who gives a shit.' Miki said something in Japanese to a waitress who'd just joined her behind the bar, then looked back at Adam, a blank expression on her deathly pale face.

'Well, thanks for your time . . .' Adam waved as he moved towards the door.

'Aren't you forgetting something, guy?'

'What?'

'Your bar tab. ¥1,000 please, plus entrance fee.'

Outside on the street Adam looked up at the Bar Belle's sign. ¥1,000 for a bottle of beer? What a rip-off place! As he stood by the door, figuring out what to do next, three Japanese men in business suits walked past him and went up the stairs. They looked exactly like all the people already up there in the club, paying through the nose to sit with girls in 'sexy' fancy dress. But did the fact that no one was forcing anyone to go there make it less of a con? Did he care?

As he walked off, even more determined now to go to the Gaspanic and forget about everything for just an hour or so, he thought what he should do was come back later, much later when the girls were leaving. Maybe one of them would be able to tell him more than Miki seemed to want to. He'd seen on a sign by the entrance that the club closed at 3.00 a.m.; Adam looked at his watch – somehow the afternoon had managed to disappear and it was already seven o'clock – only eight hours to waste before he had to be back at the Bar Belle, but he was sure he could find a way of doing it . . .

Tony Grey put the phone down and looked over at his wife, sitting at the kitchen table, waiting.

Sarah Grey raised both eyebrows, nervous. 'Well?'

'They, um, they worked out what the password was and got into Adam's computer.'

'And?'

'And there was an email from Charlie . . .'

Sarah sat forward with a jolt. 'What did it say? How long have they known?'

'They found it last night, Sarah, and it's just her, apologising for not being in touch. It was sent yesterday, and Venner said they're 99 per cent sure she's the one who actually sent it.'

'What d'you mean, 99 per cent . . . ?'

'Well, there's no way of knowing for certain, is there? Not like a phone call. Seems to be in her style, Venner said, having looked at the other ones she's sent.' Tony sat down at the table. 'They've replied "from" Adam, to see what happens, and they're talking to the company she has her account with, to see if there's any way they can work out where the email came from. He said he'd let us know as soon as he had any more information.'

'Nice of him.'

'Look, it's something at least.'

Sarah shook her head. 'Did you check with the Barretts . . . anything else from Adam?'

'Suzy's dad, Chris, he said he'd call if anything else came in.'

'What about our email, have you looked at that?'

'He's not going to be sending *us* any messages. We're not supposed to know he's gone anywhere.'

'I'm going to kill him when he gets home – what does he think he's up to, Tony?'

'I told you what Suzy said. He thought no one was doing anything, that we were just sitting round thinking Charlie was dead and not trying to find her.' Tony got up. 'Want a cup of coffee? I'm parched.'

'Tea, please . . .' Sarah stared out of the window, her face seeming to shiver, almost like a badly tuned TV picture, ready to fall apart. 'D'you think he's right? That we haven't been trying hard enough to find her? I still want to kill the little shit for taking off without saying anything, but if he's right I'm sort of glad he's there . . . that *someone's* there . . .'

'No, I don't think he's right, but I know what you mean about someone being there. I just hope he's being careful . . .'

Before making his way to the Gaspanic, Adam had gone in search of an Internet café. He wanted to send Suzy another email, not that there was a whole lot to tell her, but he needed to download to someone about what had happened, about Alice running away and that what she'd said about Charlie leaving the club with a customer possibly not being true.

Tucked away on the second floor of a narrow building on the Higashi-dori he found what he wanted. The place was like a corridor, with a line of keyboards and flat screens, a wall of vending machines and a bored-looking man sitting behind a desk, smoking and taking the money. Adam paid and took one of the spare seats, logging on and checking his email. No reply from Suzy. Odd . . . what made her life so busy she couldn't take a moment to say even just hi? Whatever. He wrote a quick résumé of his day, sent it and left.

Coming out of the Internet café he realised he was hungry, that if he didn't eat something he'd get rat-arsed the moment he started drinking. Not a good plan. Not if he still wanted to be in fairly reasonable condition at three in the morning. Opposite, just down the street, he could see a set of golden arches all lit up but didn't want any more of that, and he knew there was an English pub quite nearby that he'd passed earlier, noticing its sign outside advertising 'fish'n'chips, ham'n'eggs & welsh rabbit'. Somehow, no.

Walking down the street he spotted a noodle bar and stopped outside. Perfect . . . when in Japan, eat Japanese fast food. The place turned out to be part vending machine, part restaurant, but as there were no instructions in English, Adam had to hang around for what seemed like for ever, watching other customers, until he worked out how the system operated and felt he had a better than good chance of getting the dish he wanted.

Once he got his plate, it took almost less time to eat the meal than he'd spent trying to figure out how to make a purchase, but the meatballs and thick noodles in a kind of spicy soup were both tasty and filling and he felt ready for some down time. He deserved at least a bit of R&R.

*　　*　　*

The Gaspanic was a dive, like the guide had said, but it was a dive that certainly knew how to cook. Ten thirty and the place was already packed, loud and so smoky Adam felt like he'd had half a pack without lighting a single cigarette.

Adam was on his third, maybe fourth beer, and was with a group of Canadian backpackers, en route for Goa he seemed to remember one of them saying. They were friendly, they were funny and they were buying rounds; he was enjoying himself, more relaxed than he'd felt since Alice had called, what, ten, or was it eleven days ago? One or the other.

About 11:15 he found himself surrounded by a mixture of Americans and South Africans. He bought them a round because it seemed like the decent thing to do and then he found himself with two beers in each hand because he'd won a competition for the person whose name meant something in Japanese when you said it backwards. Adam – or *mada*, which someone told him meant 'not ready' – didn't even realise there'd *been* a competition.

This was when he completely lost track of time and some guy, whose name he thought might be Tommy or Timmy or maybe Frank, introduced him to another guy, this one Japanese, called possibly Itchy. The music was very loud, very buzzy and he wasn't really concentrating. Anyway, this Itchy bloke was with another group of people and Adam joined them because they were laughing a lot and there was this one Japanese girl who was SO pretty Adam thought she was AMAZING. Really! She seemed to like him too, but as, from what he could make out, she didn't speak English, it was difficult to be *absolutely* sure. Then his four beers had gone, he didn't know exactly where, and Itchy, was that his name? Nice man, anyway, because he gave him another one.

There was something he was supposed to be doing, Adam was sure there was, but for the life of him he couldn't remember what it might be; couldn't have been *that* important, right?

The cordless handset had been on the arm of the chair Tony was sitting in as he watched the early evening news. When it started to ring he jumped, and only just stopped it from falling on to the floor.

'Hello, 2671.'

'Tony? Chris Barrett, Suzy's dad.'

'Right, Chris . . . hello . . .'

'Thought you'd want to know, Suzy's had another email from Adam. I told her, pain of death, she had to tell me the moment she got one.'

'What does it say?'

'She's just printing it off – d'you want me to get her to forward it to you as well?'

'Could you?'

'Soon as we've finished. She hasn't emailed him, like we said, so he doesn't know the game's up yet. What are you – oh, here's Suzy . . .'

Tony heard muffled voices at the other end of the line and could hear the thump of his heart, beating in his ears. 'Chris?'

'Sorry, Tony, I've got it . . .' Papers rustled. 'He says, *"Hi Suzy, weird day today. I saw Alice and she saw me, but she ran away. Totally not what I expected . . . "* Alice is your daughter's friend, right, the one who phoned?'

147

'Yeah, the one who told us about Charlie.' Tony looked round for the remote that would let him turn down the sound on the TV but couldn't find it; he stood up. 'What else does he say?'

'It goes on, *"And I finally found the club where they were both working and the kind of manager there told me Charlie never left the place with a customer, that Alice was lying, Suzy."*' Chris cleared his throat. '*"She says that Alice and Charlie both didn't show up for work around the same time, and she hasn't seen Steve, Alice's boyfriend, since then either. She says that's what she told the police when they came round. Like I said, weird day. More later, Love A."*'

'That's it?'

'Yeah.'

Tony looked at the images on the TV screen without really seeing them. 'What the hell's going on over there?'

22

Cute in accessory

Adam woke as he rolled over. Strange how you did that, shift from oblivion to a degree of awareness, as if a page had been turned; he lay on his side with his eyes still closed, and breathed in deeply. This wasn't the kick-start he got some mornings, going from dead-to-the-world to up'n'at'em in a split second; today it was more like the slow, laborious process of bringing an awkward, complex machine to life bit by bit. No rushing, didn't want to break anything . . .

He was aware of a buzzing in his ears, the kind of thing he got after a night of loud, bass-heavy music. Then he remembered he wasn't in London and hadn't been out at a gig the night before.

He was in Tokyo.

He opened his eyes. But where in Tokyo?

Adam stared at the cream-coloured wall an arm's reach away and tried to put all the vid clips and sound samples scattered around his brain into some kind of cohesive order before he did anything like sit up and admit he really was awake. The club . . . he remembered that. The Gaspanic. Beer. Lots of very friendly people, Canadians, guys from South Africa and the States, even some actual Japanese.

More beer. Music, dancing.

Lying in this bed he didn't remember getting into – had he managed to somehow find his way back to the New Economy? – Adam caught a scent and flashed on a mental image of a smiling face, pale, heart-shaped, framed with the straightest, blackest hair. The girl in the club. He turned over on to his back.

The girl in the club. Sitting up, legs underneath her and leaning back against the wall of the room, looking down at him. Smiling.

Adam blinked and did a real cartoon double-take. 'Uh . . . ? Oh, hi . . .'

'*Kakko í!*'

'Right . . .' Adam was suddenly aware the girl was wearing a short, skimpy white vest with the words IT'S ABOUT TIME! screen-printed in blood-red on it. And nothing else. He pushed himself backwards, sat up and rubbed his stubbled chin; what next? He remembered embarrassingly little about last night – he glanced down at his watch, and this morning – and if she'd told him her name he'd forgotten what it was. He pointed at his chest. 'Adam.'

She nodded, smiling, and patted herself with her right hand. 'Aiko.'

'OK.' Adam nodded, looking around the tiny room he'd woken up in. 'Aiko . . . nice name, short and sweet . . .' He turned back to the girl, noticing that one of the shoulders of her vest had fallen down, exposing part of her breast. 'D'you, um, like speak English at all, Aiko?'

'*Engrish?*' Aiko shook her head; the vest fell further down, a crescent of dark brown skin slowly appearing. '*Le.*'

'That'll be a no, then . . .' Adam knew he was staring. '. . . jeez, wonder how the bloody hell I managed to negotiate myself back here?' He dragged his eyes away, noticing an untidy pile of clothes on the floor next to the bed. His clothes. All of them, it looked like, as he wasn't wearing a damn thing under the sheets. So . . . OK . . . him and this really fit girl, in bed, together. And so far he couldn't remember anything. He couldn't remember if they'd done it, and if they had whether he'd been a total disappointment cos of all the beer. That had never happened to him before, but he'd never been so amnesiac drunk in his life, though, weirdly enough, he didn't seem to have a hangover or anything. He heard Aiko say something and focused back on her.

'Sorry, was miles away . . .'

'*Toire ni ikitai no, óké?*' Aiko was nodding and smiling and moving down to the end of the bed. '*Chotto matte . . .*'

He watched her stand up and go to the bedroom door, gaze fixed on her perfect, tiny backside. Aiko opened the door and walked across the narrow hallway into the bathroom opposite, closing that door behind her. Leaving him on his own. Adam tried to stop smiling but he couldn't.

He didn't know where he was, or, really, who he was with, and for a couple of seconds he didn't care, he just wanted to see this girl again. See what happened next. Then his brain launched a reality check sub-program and the mirage faded. He was in Japan to try and find Charlie, not screw around with someone he'd just met in a bar, and anyway, there was Suzy. Back home, thousands of miles away. In England.

Across the hall he heard the toilet flush and realised he needed a piss pretty badly himself. Taps ran and stopped, then the bathroom door opened and Aiko was there, smiling at him.

She pointed at something he couldn't see. '*Anata mo iku?*'

'Me, go to the loo?' Or was she asking him to take a bath with her? Only one way to find out. 'Yeah, please . . .' But did he, like her, disregard the clothes thing and not even put his underpants on? Balancing on one leg, trying to get the other one in a small hole never made you look very cool – and then, was there anyone else in the house, or the flat or wherever they were? She didn't seem to mind strolling about half naked, but . . . he saw Aiko reach behind the door and then she was throwing him a towel. The girl might not be able to speak English, but she could definitely read minds.

Adam sat on the toilet in the compact bathroom, so compact it didn't have a bath, just a shower cubicle and only about a square metre or so of floor space. What should he do? Have a quick wash, get dressed and get back on the job . . . he snorted at the unintended double entendre, the kind of gag Andy often spent his entire time, back home, trying to work into conversations. Jesus, he missed Andy. He was the perfect person to just sit round with and do totally nothing, and Adam wondered what he'd think of his current situation, what advice he might have. Probably nothing useful, Andy being no more an experienced man of the world than he was.

Relying on what Andy might or might not tell him wasn't the way to go here, and he knew it. He should simply get dressed and get out. He had work to do. And she – Aiko – didn't speak a bloody word of English, so he could hardly claim, later, that this had been a meeting of minds . . . although he wished he could remember more about whether it had already been a meeting of bodies. Stop it, stop it!

He got up, flushed and stepped over to the sink. Looking at himself in the mirror, kind of sideways, as he washed his hands and face, he had no idea what he was thinking, what he was going to do. Running the water hot he soaped and rinsed his armpits. No point in leaving the house smelly, right? Or going back to bed with rank pits. He dried himself off on the towel. Anyway, for all he knew Aiko would be dressed by the time he went back to the room.

As he was wrapping the damp towel round his waist Adam saw a scrunched-up tube of toothpaste on a glass shelf under the mirror; hitching the terry cloth so it wouldn't fall down he squeezed a blob of paste on his finger and scrubbed his teeth as best he could. He didn't look at himself while he did it as he didn't want to have to answer the question, why couldn't he just buy some chewing gum from a shop when he left?

Wiping his hands on his thighs he opened the bathroom door. Aiko hadn't got dressed. She was back in bed and wearing nothing but her smile, the white cotton vest lying on top of the covers. Adam glanced down the short corridor – no one there – before stepping across the hall into the bedroom, shutting the door; whatever he ended up doing, he told himself, he had to go back in to get his clothes. As the door clicked behind him his towel came loose and fell to the floor.

Aiko's smile got bigger and she laughed.

Adam almost picked the towel up – a girl laughing when everything was revealed did nothing to bolster your self-confidence – and then saw Aiko pulling back the covers and beckoning him.

The siren's silent call. And with no mast to tie himself to, Adam hadn't got a chance. Aiko was beautiful, quite wonderful, and he could hear Andy's voice whispering in his ear, saying . . . *it'd be total bad manners to turn her down, mate* . . . and honestly, no matter how hard he tried, as he took the two steps to the bed, he couldn't think of one good reason why he should.

And this time he was going to remember absolutely everything.

Tony Grey's eyes snapped open. He peered at the clock on his bedside table . . . 6:55, a quarter of an hour before his alarm normally went off. He swore quietly, closing his eyes again and pulling the duvet over his head. He hadn't set the alarm because he wasn't going to work and, after a night like last night, knowing he was going to wake up feeling crap, he'd hoped he could sleep in.

They'd argued like they never had before, last night, he and Sarah. One of those stupid things where, because you were both so emotional, you couldn't see that you were actually on the same side of the fence – a *'you said – no I bloody didn't!'* situation that can so easily go from bad to divorce because no one wants to back down and the word sorry mysteriously vanishes from the English language.

Lying there, re-running some of the more choice moments before, some time after two a.m., they'd called a truce, Tony frowned. Something was different, missing. The quiet reassurance of another person's breathing. He looked to his left and saw the other side of the bed was empty.

He sat up. Had Sarah been so pissed off with him that she'd gone off to the spare room? Bleary-eyed he got out of bed, shuffled into his slippers, fumbled on a bathrobe from a collection that lived on the back of the door and went out on to the landing.

'Sarah?'

Silence. He stood, listening, as he tied the belt on the robe, feeling uncomfortable and not knowing quite why. Then the pad of feet and Badger appeared at Adam's bedroom door, tail wagging. Tony snapped his fingers and the dog sauntered over and sat by him to have his ears tickled. Sometimes a dog's life was definitely preferable to the complications of being a parent and a husband and a bloke, three things, judging by some of last night's comments, Sarah didn't think he was much cop at.

It had all boiled down to *when* they should get tickets to Tokyo, not *whether* – although somehow he'd ended up being the cheapskate bastard who was prepared to wait at home and see what happened to his kids. He knew he was taking the full blast of the anger, stress and emotion that Sarah had built up over her parents, that it wasn't a rational argument they were having. Grangie had finally been taken into the hospice and the sense of guilty relief Sarah felt was almost tangible. Someone else was dealing with the problem now and the focus of her concerns could turn to the children. It was totally understandable she wanted to make up for lost time, just hard to feel you were the whipping boy for all her pent-up frustrations.

Tony looked down at the blissed-out dog. 'Have you seen her, Badger?'

'Has he seen who?'

'Jesus, Sarah!' Tony jumped backwards. 'Where were you?'

'In the study.'

'All night?'

'All night? Don't be silly – you said to leave booking the tickets till the morning, remember? I woke up at half past five, six o'clock, and couldn't get back to sleep . . . it was morning, so I booked them. We fly out 9:00 a.m. Sunday. First flights I could get. OK?'

'Yeah . . . fine, absolutely fine.'

'Tony?'

'What?'

'Sorry for being a shit last night . . .'

'S'OK.'

'And Tony?'

'Yeah?'

'Why are you wearing my bathrobe?'

23

Nudy boy

It was about five o'clock when Adam and Aiko finally left the bedroom. After an essential, cramped, arousing, hilarious shower in a space designed to fit one regular-sized Japanese person, and not an extra almost-six-foot English bloke, they got dressed. In search of a hairdryer – Adam's miming skills were improving by the second – they went down the corridor to the main part of the flat. When Aiko had drawn the curtains he'd looked out of the window and discovered they were three floors up in a really massive apartment block, although he still had no idea exactly where.

Aiko went into the living space first, sort of pulling Adam after her. Like everything else he'd seen so far, the actual physical dimensions of the place were kind of scaled down from what he was used to – ceilings lower, even though he wasn't wearing shoes, and with stuff cleverly built-in to save space – but the furniture was still normal size. The effect was almost like you'd grown in your sleep.

Sitting on a small red two-seater sofa was the Japanese guy he'd met at the bar, longish blond-streaked, hair, glasses and a small, wispy beard – Itchy? Was that his name? As they walked in he and Aiko burst into conversation, the guy making a big thing of looking at his watch, tapping it and laughing. Adam just stood there, knowing he was the probable subject, because he thought he heard his name a couple of times. He wondered how much detail was being given over.

He took advantage of the moment to scan the rest of the flat and saw, off to his left, a narrow kitchen area tidily filled with utensils and cupboards and crockery; to his right there was another room with a blond wood table and six chairs, crammed bookcases lining all the walls he could see. Everything neat, in its place. But then, he supposed, it would have to be, otherwise it would be chaos. Like his own room back home. In fact, you could probably fit this entire flat into half their downstairs floor space in London . . .

Behind him he heard keys in a lock and a door opening. He looked round and saw a Japanese girl come in, taking off her shoes and pushing on what looked like shiny silk slippers. Electric blue. She came into the room carrying a large paper carrier bag, smiling and doing a nodding bow in his direction; Adam found himself bowing in return. The conversation now racked up in volume. More laughs, the occasional glance in his direction and all the time Aiko was holding his hand, loose, natural, stroking his palm lazily with her little finger.

In the middle of it all Adam heard the warbling ring tone of a mobile. The girl who'd just arrived took a flip phone out of her pocket – complete with a handful of tiny, furry creatures and a couple of metallic badges hanging from it – and answered, including Aiko in the discussion with whoever was calling.

'You OK?'

For a second Adam wondered if he'd somehow learnt

Japanese and could understand what was being said, and then he realised the man — he looked older than him, but it was hard to tell — was speaking to him. In English.

'Me? Yeah, I'm, um . . . I'm fine, great.'

'Some night, las' night, yeah?'

Adam nodded. 'You could say . . . to be honest, right? I don't remember too much about how I got here, you know?' Adam glanced at Aiko. 'Where the hell am I anyway?'

'Edge of town, man, nex' stop is outside city limit.'

'Did we drive or what?'

'No car, man, way too spensive; we came on train.'

'Come to where? I mean, where am I?'

'You never heard of it, man, Rokugodote . . .' The man laughed, big smile, lots of teeth. 'Like a place people live, but tourist don't go visit, OK?'

'Yeah . . .' Adam felt Aiko drop his hand and he saw she was taking the phone the other girl was offering.

'Aiko say you call Adam, like first man, tha right?'

Adam nodded. 'Yeah . . . and what's your name? I've got a bit of a blank about last night.'

'Me? Kenichi, an tha's Ayumi.' He pointed to the other girl, and she smiled at the mention of her name. 'She an Aiko? You know, man, they bes fren.'

'You speak pretty good English, Kenichi.'

'I speak lika dam ugly dog, man! No pretty . . .' He grinned and shook his head. 'Take seat, man, they gonna be long — *fuku* . . .' he pulled at his shirt, 'clowz stuff, you know?'

'Yeah, I know.' Adam sat in an armchair next to the sofa. 'Not many people here seem to speak much English, where'd you learn?'

'Music, man . . . CD. I work at Tower, near Shibuya crossing? Listen to stuff all day, read, you know, stuff inside.

159

Ayumi, she like design shoe and stuff, like acca-sessory, an she kinda sing ina band, right?' Kenichi picked up a pack of cigarettes from the low table in front of him, showed it to Adam, who shook his head, and then lit one. 'You here doing vacation, man?'

'No . . . I came to try and find my sister, Charlie . . . Charlotte.' Adam sat forward. He suddenly really wanted to ask for a cigarette; he was beginning to feel twitchy about what he was doing – or rather, *not* doing. He was sitting in some flat, not out looking for Charlie. And then his brain let loose a previously locked-up memory and he remembered he hadn't gone back to the Bar Belle when it closed to try and talk to the hostesses. He sat back and swore under his breath.

'You OK, man?'

'No, not really, I'm screwing up, big time . . . I shouldn't be here.'

'You don't got wife an kids, man,' Kenichi smiled. 'No ring on finger, right?'

'It's nothing like that . . .' He could just hear Andy saying, *'I think Suzy might disagree with you here . . . '* 'My, uh, my sister was working in a club, and then she went missing . . . and now so's her friend, sort of. It was in all the papers back home, maybe even here, I don't know.' Kenichi shrugged; either he hadn't seen the story or he didn't understand what Adam was saying. 'Basically, I came to Tokyo to try and find my sister.'

'You tole Aiko?'

Adam looked up at Aiko, who'd now given the phone back to Ayumi, and she smiled at him. He was about to answer when she started talking, not to him, but Kenichi. It sounded emphatic, like she was making a demand of some kind. 'What did she say?'

'Oh, jus I have to tell you Aiko an Ayumi be finish soon, an sorry.' Kenichi stubbed out his cigarette in an ashtray with half a dozen butts already in it.

'OK . . .' It was Adam's turn to shrug. 'And, no, I haven't told her about my sister cos I have no idea what the sign language for "kidnapped" is . . . maybe you can save us both a lot of time and tell her for me.'

'Sure, maybe . . . maybe later.' Kenichi looked at his watch and said something to Ayumi, who nodded. 'It's time we went to baths – you gonna come, man, right?'

Adam frowned. Baths? They'd just had a shower. Or did he mean go swimming? He looked questioningly up at Aiko, who seemed about to go off with Ayumi; she came straight over, knelt by the chair, locked eyes with him and spoke a few words in Japanese. Then she kissed him, one of those long ones, very long ones that were more than just a kiss, and then said something to Kenichi before she got up and went after Ayumi.

'You like her, man?'

'What's not to like?' Adam saw Kenichi frown and look puzzled. 'Yeah, I like her a lot, really a lot.'

'Aiko like you really a lot also, man.' Kenichi, nodded, lighting up another cigarette. 'She is *kubittake* . . . ah, neck length, man.'

'*Neck* length?'

'Sure.'

'And that means?'

'Like I say, she go for you, man. Big time.'

It turned out that Kenichi really had meant they were going to have a bath, not a swim. He told Adam, as they left the apartment, that he and Ayumi often went to the public bath house on a Friday, then on to a restaurant. A way to get rid of the week, he said, in the salt waters. Adam figured he meant mineral, like some kind of spa.

They got to the place after quite a short walk through narrow streets in single-file – inches from a constant rattle and hum of cars, trucks, scooters and bikes – as there were no pavements, just a white line on the tarmac. When they arrived, Adam thought the public baths, which were clean, but slightly run-down, looked like photos of his local swimming pool he'd seen when he was a kid, before the council had spent gazillions tarting it up. At the entrance, where you paid, they split up, Adam assuming they were going to different changing rooms.

'OK, I tell you wha to do.' Kenichi opened the door and let Adam through, handing him a towel out of the bag he was carrying. 'Firs, man, you gotta wash, soap it up, head down to foot, OK? Then shower, *then* you get in baths. Watch me, man, OK?'

The bath house was segregated, the girls the other side of a white-tiled wall that didn't quite reach the glass roof, and Adam was in a room full of naked men – no swimming trunks here – some sitting on tiny plastic stools under showers, knees up around their ears, washing, shaving, rinsing, others walking around shooting the breeze. No one had given him a second glance, even the two small kids, a boy and a girl, who'd been there with their dad when he and Kenichi had arrived. Strange, he thought, because it didn't look like the kind of place that got a lot of visiting *gaijin* customers.

Adam was sitting up to his neck in hot, steaming, bubbling water the colour of full-strength Coca-Cola; it smelled slightly peaty, organic. Opposite him, Kenichi, with his hair pulled back into a ponytail, sat with his head leaning on the rim of the wooden tub and his eyes closed. He looked very Zen. They'd both been in this particular tub for about five minutes and he had to admit it was very relaxing, even though, on the way to the baths, he'd begun to stress about getting back to Tokyo so he could be outside the Bar Belle. He really should've been there the night before and he felt bad, but the hot water was easing the tension from his shoulders and the angst kind of drifted out of his head with the steam.

He really had to get back to Tokyo anyway. He had a room booked at the New Economy and didn't want to lose it by not turning up for another night . . . Being with Aiko was making it very difficult to think straight. And he was also hungry like a wolf. He'd get Kenichi to explain everything to Aiko over the meal they were going to have after finishing at the baths; she'd understand that, no matter how much he liked her, and he hadn't been lying when he'd told Kenichi he liked her really a lot, he *had* to get back to trying to find Charlie. Otherwise he was just pissing about and he knew he didn't want that thought hanging over his head the rest of his life.

And what about Aiko?

Big, big question. Was it just sex? The sex had been majestic, no doubt about that, but they did also seem to connect on a whole other level that wasn't physical at all. It sounded stupidly cosmic even inside his head, let alone if he ever actually got to say it out loud. They didn't speak a word of each other's language, but the fact was he felt a strong contact, almost a bond between them . . . and not forgetting, she was beautiful. Small but perfectly formed, to use one of his dad's favourite phrases. And the feelings appeared to be mutual. Aiko must've seen *something* other than a drunk scally at the Gaspanic to want to take him home to bed. Could you fall in love this fast? *Was* she in love with him? That kiss, just before they'd left the apartment, had been about as different as a kiss could be.

Was *he* in love with Aiko? Right now he was beginning to think the answer was yes, but if that was true what about Suzy . . . didn't he love her? Yesterday he'd have probably said yeah, he did, even though she was right and he did expect more from her than he got. More emotion. Like Aiko . . .

God, he was confused.

'We get out now, man,' Adam jumped, looking across the tub at Kenichi, who was holding up a hand wrinkled like a prune and laughing, 'else we gonna look all like *toshiyori* . . . you know, old guy – Aiko no like you like that!'

'Kenichi . . . ?'

'Yeah, man?'

'You known Aiko long?'

'Couple years. Ayumi work for Aiko father, met her that way.'

'What's he do?'

'Fashion, man . . . gotta fashion company.'

'And she really likes me?'

'Aiko? She win lottery, man!'

Adam stood up, shivering slightly in the cooler air. 'Lottery?'

'Get a boy like you, with a blond hair an stuff? *Big* win, man.'

164

24

It's a labour of human . . .

The restaurant they took him to was a cab ride away; Adam in the back between Aiko and Ayumi, Kenichi up front. A smart, lime-green, 70s-style saloon, it wasn't like any cab he'd ever been in before; for a start, the passenger doors opened and closed automatically, and then the seats all had dainty white lace covers on the head restraints and the driver wore white cotton gloves. Light years away from the skanky north London minicabs he and his mates used, rust buckets with saggy seats, smelling of stale fags and rattling like a tin can full of nuts and bolts.

When the cab got to the restaurant, Kenichi refused any money from Adam and he was taken to a narrow, wooden-fronted place that looked like the kind of restaurant you'd only go to if you knew about it. Inside there were only about eight tables, heavy, red-stained pine with red vinyl banquette seats and padded stools; kind of rustic, in a completely foreign way. Square paper lamp shades hung down from the ceilings and the walls were covered in a haphazard collection of what looked like framed family snapshots. They took a table at the back of the restaurant where there was a view right into the kitchen.

'This place good for *sakana*.' Kenichi weaved his hand, palm upright, through the air towards Adam. 'You know, man . . .'

'Fish?'

'Yeah, man, fish!' Kenichi nodded, grinning. He pointed with his thumb at the kitchen where Adam could see the back of someone moving efficiently between sink, chopping block and a big wok. 'No *sashimi*, Mr Suzuki do great cooking, jus him there.'

'*Sashimi*?'

'Raw, man.'

A small, round woman with a flat, impassive face appeared out of the kitchen, a smile blossoming as soon as she saw Kenichi, Ayumi and Aiko. They introduced her to Adam – which involved serial bowing – and he gathered that this was Mrs Suzuki, who handled everything front of house while her husband cooked. Tall, cold beers were delivered moments later and food ordered; no menus, just a general to-and-fro discussion.

'You like everythin, man?'

'I'm so hungry, you put it on a plate and I'll eat it.'

Adam watched Kenichi translate what he'd just said – lots of nodding, glances in his direction and laughing – then Mrs Suzuki asked something.

'You eat *tako*?' Kenichi made his hand into a cone shape and waggled his fingers. 'Got lotta legs, man . . .'

'Octopus?' Adam nodded at Mrs Suziki. 'Yeah, I eat that.'

Mrs Suzuki left and everyone took a drink; in the silence Adam became aware of the buzz of relaxed conversation in the easy atmosphere around him, like being in someone's house. It was great here, with these people . . . with Aiko next to him, their arms touching.

'Kenichi?'

He looked over. 'Yeah, man?'

'You told Aiko about my sister yet?'

Kenichi glanced at Aiko, then back to Adam. 'No yet, man . . .' He directed a volley of Japanese at Aiko and Adam felt the atmosphere subtly change. Aiko took his hand in both of hers and spoke to Ayumi and Kenichi, lacing her fingers with his. Then she looked at him, a kind of worried, embarrassed expression on her face.

'What?' Adam had no idea what was going on, but was beginning to realise that Kenichi had an opinion about something to do with Aiko, a bone to pick? He didn't know. And Aiko was confused about the situation, asking Ayumi stuff, Kenichi shrugging, as if to say 'it's up to you'. Was this anything to do with him? 'Kenichi . . . ?'

Kenichi shrugged and lit a cigarette. Looking up at the ceiling he blew a smoke ring. 'You tell him, man.'

You tell him? Tell who? 'What d'you mean?' Adam knew there was a language barrier here, but . . .

'He means I tell you that I speak Engrish, Adam.'

Adam did his second double-take of the day.

'It was game . . . jus for fun.' Aiko let go of Adam's hand and looked away, then down at the table. 'Started last night at club.' She shot him a glance. 'You mad at me?'

'Mad? I, uh . . . *you speak English?*' Aiko nodded, eyes down. He didn't know what to say. Had this all been just one big joke on him, or what? Adam looked over at Kenichi and Ayumi, neither of whom were laughing. OK . . . but did the fact that Aiko had been playing a trick change the way he felt about her . . . had she also been pretending that this was anything more than a fast-food relationship? 'Was, like, um, *everything* a game?'

'You an me?'

'Yeah, you and me . . . was all that just for fun too?' Adam reached across the space there was now between them and touched Aiko's hand. 'I mean, it's kind of OK if it was, cos it was a lot of fun, but I thought . . .'

'No just fun for me, Adam, honest. Sorry.' Aiko crossed her hands on her chest. 'You forgive?'

Before Adam could say anything Mrs Suzuki swept out of the kitchen carrying a tray covered in bowls of steaming food and set them, one by one, down on the table, along with chopsticks and paper napkins.

'Yeah . . .' He broke apart a pair of wooden chopsticks, grinning. 'I forgive.'

'Hot-dam!' Kenichi stubbed out his cigarette. 'I like happy ending, man!'

With the truth out and the game over, the only person who needed translations now was Ayumi, who spoke about as much English as Adam spoke Japanese. While they ate, Adam laid out the basic story of Charlie's disappearance and how he came to be in Tokyo trying to find out what had happened to her. Everything except Suzy. Way too complicated, that, definitely a situation to be dealt with at some other time. *No need to stir up the situation, eh, mate?* Andy's voice whispered in his ear.

Pushing the nagging reminders that he had another life away and locking the door on them, Adam also explained about having to get back to Tokyo that night so he could try and catch the girls coming out of the Bar Belle – and that he had to contact the New Economy Hotel or he'd have to go and stay in a capsule hotel again.

'No way, Adam!' Aiko's loaded chopsticks stopped in midair. 'You don't need hotel or anything!'

'You taking him home, man?' Kenichi looked over at Adam and winked. 'You see the movie *Meet Parents*? Her father lotta fun, like de Niro, man!'

'Don't listen, Adam, my father sure very nice man; but my friend Keiko has place, near Harajuku, more central . . .' Aiko got out her mobile, which had even more stuff hanging off it than Ayumi's, and flipped it open.

'But I booked this hotel for five days, Aiko.'

'You don't wanna stay with me?'

Stay with Aiko? OK . . . 'Yeah, course I do, but what about your parents and stuff? They won't want to know where you are?'

'They away, gone to USA for two week; they don't know nothing.' Aiko tapped in a series of numbers and put the handset to her ear, waiting for the call to be picked up.

Adam watched as Aiko burst into high-speed Japanese, then looked over at Kenichi, raising his eyebrows. 'All Japanese girls like this?'

Kenichi grinned and shook his head. 'No way, man . . . you got one special type girl. Very unique, man, lemme tell you.'

'What's she saying to her friend?'

'Keiko finding out she got guest tonight, man. No hotel for you – what I told you, right? You Euro-boy, the girl they *love* you, man!'

'Her friend, is she gonna mind?'

'Don't got no choice, man, know why-mean?'

'I think I do.' Adam smiled, sitting back. 'How come you're not, like working today, Kenichi?'

'I gotta do *Nichiyobi*, man.' He made one hand leap frog over the other. 'You know, not tomorrow, nex day?'

'Sunday?'

'Right. So, no work today.'

Aiko closed the phone and nodded firmly, looking at her

watch. 'Fixed, but we better be in a hurry.'

'Hurry, why?' Adam checked his watch: 10:30, not what you'd call late.

'Lot of stuff to do . . .'

An hour later they were on a train, speeding back towards Tokyo. They'd had to get a cab back to Kenichi and Ayumi's apartment, collect all Aiko's stuff, walk to the station – too close to waste time waiting for another cab – and then wait for a train that would take them back to central Tokyo. Out here, so far from the middle of town, there were no signs in English and Adam knew he'd stay lost for ever without Aiko.

The plan, it turned out, was to get to Roppongi, where Adam discovered Aiko had left her scooter; from there it wasn't far to her friend Keiko's apartment. They'd go there, settle in and then, around two thirty, go back to Roppongi and be outside the Bar Belle when the girls came out. Simple.

It was, thought Adam, like having a tour manager to sort everything out for him. Nice. Not long after the train left the station it went over a river and across a flat stretch of ground; a couple of hundred metres away, under what looked like another elevated track, he saw a series of flickering lights and the silhouetted shapes of people moving, like an encampment.

He pointed out of the window. 'What's that?'

'They got no home, no job . . . live there now, like up in Ueno.'

'Ueno?'

'Big park near National Museum, whole like city there . . .'

Adam hadn't been aware of seeing homeless people on the streets. Not like you saw them back in London, where they seemed to be clinging to life in the shadows of almost every other doorway, hanging round all the cashpoints, reminding even people like him that they really did have spare change. Spare change . . . jeez, he even had plastic, not much in the way of credit, but something. And a home.

'You OK, Adam?'

'Yeah, fine . . . just thinking about my parents . . .'

DS Keith Venner put the phone down, sat back and pushed the fingers of both hands through his hair. 'That was Mr Grey.'

DC Eddy Thomson looked up. 'What'd he say?'

'He and his good lady wife are on the first flight out to Tokyo on Sunday . . . *sayonara*, and thanks for all the sushi.'

'What?'

'Nothing, Eddy, I'm just rambling.' Venner reached out and picked up his now tepid cup of coffee.

'That it, boss?'

'Sorry?'

'He say anything else?'

'Yeah, he said their boy had emailed his girlfriend again. Claims the person running the place the sister was working in says the friend was lying, that the sister never left the bar or whatever with any customer. But then they would, wouldn't they.'

'Anyone managed to find out where the sister sent that email from yet?'

'Not yet, Eddy; I made a call, asked for Simons to be kept informed, not much else any of us can do at the moment.' Venner took a sip of coffee and made a face. 'Cold . . . anyway, we're out of the loop on this one, we only know what

Interpol or the Foreign Office remember to tell us.'

'And the parents.'

'Yeah, and the parents . . .'

'Not a good look, though, is it? She's been missing almost two weeks now, the girl.'

'There's no rules to these things, Eddy, no actual Law of Diminishing Returns if you don't find them in the first forty-eight hours. She could turn up any time.'

'Yeah, turn up dead.' Eddy Thomson picked up the cap of a blue biro and chewed on it. 'I was them, I'd've been out there straight away, not leave it this long. Two weeks? I'm not surprised the boy took off and went over there. That would've been me, in his shoes.'

'Which you would *not* want to be in when he gets back!'

'Least he's doing something, boss.'

'If I was them, right? I don't know that I'd let *my* daughter go off round the world with another girl in the first place. There's enough bloody lunatics wandering about this neck of the woods to worry about, without the shit going on elsewhere.'

'You're a cop, boss, you can't help but see the shit side of everything.'

'You're beginning to sound just like my wife, Eddy.'

'Now there's a worry, boss . . .'

172

25

I feel you

'Your parents really not know you here, Adam?' Aiko looked at Adam and he shook his head. 'You should call.'

'Yeah . . . maybe.'

'What time is in London now?'

Adam checked the dual time on his watch. 'Quarter to four in the afternoon.'

'So you call when we get to Keiko's, still time.'

'Look . . . they know I'm away, but they don't know I'm here in Tokyo. They *think* I'm staying somewhere. With a friend.' Adam shifted in his seat, unease making his skin feel itchy . . . his parents thought he was away somewhere with his *girl*friend. Was now the time to bring this fact out of the bag, or did he continue with the lie? Except, could you be lying if no one had asked you about what you were trying to hide? God, he was crap at the guilt thing. He was thousands of miles from anyone who knew anything about him, so why couldn't he just blank emotional responsibilities? Just for a few days.

The mostly empty train *diddle-dee-dee-diddle-dee-da*'d its way towards Shinagawa, where Aiko had told him they'd have to change, and they were sitting down one end of a carriage with only three other people in it. Outside the low-rise sprawl of outer-rim Tokyo spread away either side of the train, houses packed together like boxes on super-market shelves, tighter, if anything. It looked to Adam like some giant had put his arms round the city and gathered it even closer together, so that you'd have to walk sideways to get between buildings.

Watching Aiko as she got her phone out of her bag and texted someone – probably Ayumi, he thought – he felt like the tables had been turned and he was now kind of in the position Aiko had been back at the restaurant, withholding relevant information. She'd had friends to talk to, though, people there to help her to do the right thing; his subcon-scious seemed to have lumbered him with Andy-in-the-head, which was no real substitute. Andy would probably make some joke about the truth not hurting, it was just the fist smacking you in the gob that would, once you told it.

'Look, Aiko . . .' Adam, in an unconscious echo of what Aiko had done in the restaurant, took one of her hands in both of his.

'You got girlfren, right?'

A plain statement of fact. Requiring an honest yes, or a lying no. Simple. How did she do that? Know stuff?

'Yeah, but . . .'

'I got boyfren, kind of.'

A kind-of boyfriend? What kind was that?

'He was on way out, just not told him yet.'

'Oh, right . . .' Matter-of-fact, or what?

'I tex him.'

'You're going to text him? Right, OK.'

'I *have* text him, all done.'

'When?'

'Just now.' Aiko squeezed Adam's hand and smiled. Nodding.

It'd be his turn, then.

He breathed in and let it out slowly. 'I, uh, didn't come here to do *anything* but try and find Charlie, right?' Aiko nodded. God, did he sound like he was apologising, making excuses? 'I wasn't at the Gaspanic to pick anyone up, just have a drink and relax a bit, before I went back to the place Charlie and Alice worked in. And like I said, I don't remember a *whole* lot about last night, but I'm glad it happened. Really. Didn't know you could get so, ah . . . so close to someone so fast, not had time to, you know . . .' *Crap, crap, crap* – this was like a letter to an Agony Aunt! 'Look, I can't just pick up the phone and text someone, not like you just did . . . and this is all so, I dunno, so weird, not like part of my real life. Not a dream either, but I'm not supposed to even *be* here, Aiko – I'd be at college right now, if I hadn't lost my temper . . .' He stopped and looked at Aiko looking back at him, smiling. 'And yeah . . . I do like have a girlfriend too.'

'She nice? Must be pretty, right?'

'Yeah, she is, but it's not like being with you. Another girl, another planet. Entirely.' Adam shook his head, trying to rationalise his feelings, put his emotions into some kind of semblance of order so he could work out how he actually felt, and then attempt to put it all into words that didn't sound like some dumb, godawful greetings card. 'This is like being in a kind of parallel universe, Aiko, know what I mean? There's what I'm doing here, that basically only *I* know about, and then there's my life back in England. Everyone, excepting Suzy . . .' the name just slipped out, '. . . thinks that's where I am right now. And it's like both lives are happening at the same time.'

'Confuse, right?'

'100% solid.'

'That mean yes?'

Adam nodded. Confused? That didn't even scratch the surface of what he was going through. The thing that had happened with Alice, and what the woman at the Bar Belle had said, would be bad enough without also having to deal with working out how he felt about Suzy. It was weird how he could sit right next to Aiko, close, together, and think about someone else with this almost detached attitude. Is that what it would be like when he got back to London – would Aiko become a separate thing he could kind of observe in a disconnected way? Was that possible?

His thoughts were broken into by the feeling that the train was slowing down as it approached the next station. Aiko stood and picked up her bag from the seat next to her, the train's brakes beginning to squeal.

'Change here.'

Adam got up. 'How did you know?'

'Know what, Adam?'

'That I had a girlfriend?'

Aiko tiptoed and kissed him. 'Easy. You don't look kind of boy who sit around by himself too much, OK?'

The subject of boyfriends and girlfriends seemed to have been sidelined once they'd left the train at Shinagawa and changed on to the subway, and Adam couldn't say he was the least bit unhappy about that. He had no doubt that it would be back on the agenda before too long. Stuff like that didn't just go away.

They came up to street level at Roppongi station, the corner diagonally opposite where Adam had been stiffed by the club tout the first night he'd arrived and come to have a look, all of two days ago. Two days, how unbelievable was that? He found it hard to get his head round so much happening in so short a time, but there was Aiko, holding his hand, to prove it had. As she guided him off through the crowds he looked to see if the same guy was still working the same corner, but there were too many people jamming the pavements. High Touch Town was in full swing.

Aiko's scooter, a small silver Honda 125, was where she'd left it the night before, and not even chained. So wouldn't have happened back home. She opened the top box and got an open face helmet out. Adam ran his hand over a now extremely stubbled chin.

'Just the one helmet?'

'Keiko has spare, should fit.'

'Great, but what about now – you have a helmet law here, right?'

'Sorry?'

'You have to wear one of these,' Adam tapped the pink Shoei Aiko was holding, 'or the cops stop you, yeah?'

'Sure, if they see you.'

'If they see you?'

'No far – I go small roads, we be fine, Adam. Trus me.'

Like he had a choice.

The ride was intense. Aiko buzzed through a criss-cross of narrow side streets, zipping over any major roads they came to and diving back into the network of smaller roads. Adam was a good pillion – he had a couple of mates with scooters and he often got lifts from them – and he started the journey leaning back against the top box, hands loosely on Aiko's hips. But Aiko rode fast, hardly slowing for corners, making Adam hang on tight as they leant into sharp left- and right-hand bends. Not such a hardship.

It wasn't cold, even though it was now after midnight, but the wind made Adam's eyes water as he kept an obsessive watch for any police who might be on patrol. The sky was a dirty purple, the city glow masking out all but the brightest stars, and silhouetted against it a dark, tangled web of cables hung above their heads, an almost organic, jungle growth. As they sped down one street, from somewhere the scent of jasmine cut through the urban street perfume, and then was gone.

Aiko, slowing for a main junction, turned her head. 'There soon.'

'Great.'

'You OK?'

'Fine.' Adam relaxed his hold on her; sure he was fine.

'I scare you?'

'No!' Aiko twisted the accelerator, the scooter leapt across the street and Adam lurched back, his hands pulled upwards over Aiko's breasts.

She laughed, leaning back into him. 'Want me to go long way round?'

Adam stood looking out of the window of Keiko's tenth-floor flat in a nondescript, pale brick apartment block in a street full of similar buildings. In the tiny galley kitchen he could hear the girls, Aiko obviously bringing her friend up to speed with who he was and how he got to be there.

Behind him on a table was the carrier bag of stuff – a peace offering/gift of flowers for Keiko, which they'd forgotten to give her when they arrived, and toiletries for Adam. They'd bought it all at the 24-hour convenience store opposite where the scooter was parked.

Keiko – hair cut in a short, dramatic style, chic black satin trousers, silver and patent leather belt and a white blouse with the collar up – had greeted them at the door, curious and not shy about staring. Adam had felt a bit like an exhibit at a show. She looked the same age as Aiko, but dressed older, wore more make-up and had to be older to have a flat of her own. She was the manager of a clothes boutique where Aiko worked at the weekends; their parents were old friends and Keiko had, Aiko'd said, always been like a big sister to her.

He looked at his watch. Shit! Half past midnight – could he still phone the New Economy about his room, or would he have to wait now until the morning? Adam turned away from the window as the girls came out of the kitchen, giggling at something.

'You OK, Adam?'

He looked at his watch again. 'Is it too late to call the hotel?'

'Oh, sorry – forget, do it now.' Aiko flipped open her phone. 'You got number?'

Adam dug the card he'd taken from the hotel out of his wallet and handed it over, watching Aiko dial as Kieko watched him. They smiled at each other.

'Thanks for letting me stay.'

Keiko nodded a little bow. '*Dó itashimashite.*'

'OK . . .' Adam pasted a smile on and glanced away; what now? One way conversations were pretty pointless, but standing round in silence was kind of weird too . . .

'*Tókyó – ga suki des ka?* Is good?'

'Oh, yeah . . . right, um, I like Tokyo – very nice!' He smiled for real this time, looking over at Aiko, still on the phone. Like a quite a few people he'd seen, she held her hand up so you couldn't see her mouth when she talked, but he noticed she looked puzzled, frowning slightly. Keiko said something in Japanese as Aiko snapped the phone shut and she shrugged, shaking her head.

'What's wrong, Aiko?'

'Bit not right, Adam.'

'What? They have my booking, don't they?'

'Sure, sure . . . no that.'

'What then?'

'This person,' she held up her phone, 'say people been round for you. Couple times.'

'To the hotel?' Aiko nodded. 'But no one knows I'm staying there . . . and I don't know anyone in Tokyo anyway – you sure that's what they said?'

'Sure, they say someone not too good, either.' Aiko chewed her lip, eyes darting from Adam to Keiko and back. 'And they have to say *a lot* that you no there yet.'

Keiko spoke again, looking at Adam as she did so. The response was a lot of headshaking from Aiko, who then went and got the cellophane-wrapped flowers out of the carrier bag and gave them to Keiko.

'What was she saying – something about those people?'

'It was nothing . . .'

'Come on, it was something about me and those people going to the hotel.'

'OK . . .' Aiko looked at her friend, then straight up at Adam. 'She say, what do I know? Jus met you, right? Could be anybody.'

'And what'd you say?'

'Bullshit. Something like that.'

'Right . . . OK . . . so, is Keiko still happy with me staying?'

Aiko fired off a sentence, to which Keiko, unwrapping the

flowers, nodded impassively. 'She fine, Adam.'

'Just fine, or happy fine?'

Keiko went over to a built-in cupboard and took out a plain crystal vase. 'I happy . . . no probrem.'

Adam, feeling slightly awkward, hoping he wasn't trying too hard to appear like the reasonably honest, trustworthy person he thought it was fair to say he was, waved tentatively. 'Thanks . . .'

It was hard, putting yourself in someone else's shoes, but he could see why Keiko mightn't be totally delirious about him; from her point of view, who the hell was he? Adam shook his head. Why were these people asking for him at the New Economy? How did *anyone* know he was supposed to be staying there?

Did these mystery visitors turning up at the New Economy have anything to do with Charlie?

26

It's a friend wholly

The spare helmet that Keiko had eventually unearthed from the back of a closet in her bedroom – the one that had belonged to some ex-boyfriend – was a tight fit, but at least now he was legal and hadn't had to spend the entire journey back to Roppongi literally looking over his shoulder for cops.

Adam had no idea what street the Bar Belle was in – name signs, even for big main roads didn't appear to be a priority in Tokyo – but he remembered how to get back and directed Aiko pretty much straight there, with only a couple of wrong turns. She rode past the club, its sign flashing above the doorway, and came to a halt where another couple of scooters were parked up. One was a weird contraption, like nothing he'd ever seen before, and Adam dismounted and prised off his helmet off to take a closer look. 'What the hell's that?'

'Deliver noodles.'

'In the box at the back?'

Aiko nodded. 'Box go roun corner no like us . . .' she put both hands up and leant them sharply sideways, '. . . but do like this . . .' She then kept her hands vertical as she mimed them going round a bend. 'No spill, OK?'

Adam nodded, looking at his watch again: ten to three. 'Thanks for bringing me over . . . I could've taken the subway, you didn't need to come. I mean, you've got to work tomorrow, right?'

'Should do, but Keiko give me day off. Good luck for you, right?'

He went over to her, standing checking her hair in one of the scooter's wing mirrors, reached out and touched her cheek. 'Why'd you make such a big deal about coming with me tonight . . . think I need protection?'

'They see you with girl, won't think you trouble, Adam.' She looked past him, back up towards the club. 'People coming out now.'

Adam turned to see a handful of Japanese men in suits stagger out on to the street and wander off into what was left of the night. A few minutes later a couple of European girls came out and stood for a moment, lighting cigarettes.

'We go, right?' Aiko nodded towards the girls and they both started walking back up to the club's entrance.

Adam glanced back at the scooter. 'Hang on, you've left your keys in the ignition.'

'I do this too much.' Aiko went back and pulled the key and its cartoon character fob out from where it was hanging under the handlebars.

As they walked up to the two girls, one of whom was now on her mobile, a third came out of the club and stood a few feet away, leaning against the wall and looking at her watch. Aiko put her arm round Adam and hooked a thumb through one of his belt loops in a move he knew was meant to signal 'we are a couple'.

'Scuse me . . .' Three pairs of eyes swivelled to look at them. 'Hi . . . I just wondered if, um, like any of you worked with Alice and Charlie?'

The girl on the mobile turned her back on them and carried on muttering into her phone; her friend looked away as she spoke. 'Who?' Heavy accent, not English.

'Alice Reardon and Charlie Grey, English girls . . . Charlie went missing two weeks ago. Did you know them?'

The girl dropped her cigarette and stubbed it out with the toe of her shoe. 'No,' she nodded at her companion, 'new here . . . Natasha, we go.' She turned on her heels and walked off, her friend following, still on the phone.

The lie was so blatant, so like the girl couldn't give a shit whether he realised or not, that Adam was shocked, unable to say anything as a clutch of girls spilled out on to the street, like a class being let out of school, and disappeared. He looked at Aiko, making a 'What was *that* all about?' face.

'I know Charlie and Alice.'

'Sorry?' Adam looked up, not realising there was anyone left outside the Bar Belle. He saw the girl who'd come down after Natasha and her friend, still leaning against the wall.

'I go dis way.' She pushed herself off the wall and walked away down the narrow street.

'Come on.' Aiko urged Adam forward. 'She want to talk.'

It turned out Oxana, from the Ukraine, twenty-three, and at the end of a long day, wanted to drink much more than she wanted to talk. Sitting with her in a cramped, smoky bar called JoJo's, Adam had paid for three vodkas before she decided the time was right to actually say anything to him about Charlie and Alice.

'I saw you yesterday, talking to Miki.' Oxana swirled ice around the tall glass as she took a deep drag of her cigarette.

Adam nodded. 'She said Charlie didn't leave the club with a customer, like Alice told my parents.' He watched Oxana's pretty-but-hard face, fine lines radiating out from the corners of her mascara and kohl-black shadowed eyes, dark roots beginning to show in her corn-yellow hair. Cool, seen-it-all-before, not giving anything away.

'She your *gáru-frendo*?' Oxana nodded at Aiko.

'What?'

'She say am I your girlfren.'

Adam, leaning forward with both elbows on the table, smiled to himself . . . there was that subject, back again like he'd known it would be. 'Yeah . . . yeah, she is.' But time to change it. 'You speak Japanese?'

'Hostess Japanese – *uokka-tonikku o onegai shimas . . .*' she held up her now half-empty glass, ". . . *subarashí ude-dokei . . .*" She showed Adam the shiny new Rolex on her wrist. 'What you need to know?'

'So what d'you know about Charlie and Alice? Why wouldn't your friends talk to me about them?'

'They don't care, not their business.'

'Right . . . so why're *you* talking to me?'

'I see you with Miki? You look . . . alone. I know how that is too.'

'Was Miki telling me the truth about Charlie?'

Oxana nodded. 'Time Charlie went? She was no so good friend though. With Alice.'

'Why not?'

Oxana shrugged. 'Maybe Alice's new boyfriend? I think maybe that . . . not my business either.'

'New boyfriend? What happened to whatsisname, Steve?'

'Steve?' Oxana drained her glass.

'Alice's old boyfriend.'

Another shrug. 'Only saw once.'

'What was wrong with the new one? Didn't Charlie like him?'

Oxana held up her left hand, palm towards her and the little finger bent so to Adam and Aiko it looked like the top two joints were missing.

Adam shook his head, shoulders and eyebrows raised. 'And? What does that mean?'

Aiko traced a line through the condensation on one of Oxana's empty glasses. 'It mean *yakuza*, Adam.'

'*Yakuza?*'

Oxana shook the ice left in her glass. 'Mafia . . .'

They left Oxana with a fourth vodka tonic, for which she'd repaid them with the information that she'd heard Alice had moved in with this new man – she thought his name was Yoshi – somewhere in Kabukicho. Why Oxana had actually decided to tell them what she knew, Adam wasn't entirely sure – could just thinking he looked lonely be the whole reason? Whatever, it meant he now had a couple more tiny pieces of the puzzle. Some small justification, at least, for coming to Tokyo, even if he didn't feel he was any nearer to finding Charlie.

As they walked back to where the scooter was parked, drinking sweet black coffee straight out of tins they'd bought from a vending machine, Adam ran the facts in front of Aiko, trying to work out if there was anything he'd missed. He was pretty sure Charlie hadn't left the club with anyone, suspicious or otherwise; then, to add to the very sketchy picture, there was the fact that she and Alice seemed to have had a falling out of some kind, possibly over Alice's new gangster boyfriend. Something was going on, but what did it have to do with Charlie being kid-napped? *Had* Charlie been kidnapped?

'You believe Oxana, Aiko?'

'You don't?'

'Jeez, I dunno . . . she backs up what Miki told me, which means Alice must have lied.'

'She run away when she see you.'

'But why would you make up a story about someone – your best friend for crissake – being kidnapped? Because she didn't like your boyfriend? What a pile of crap.'

'Pile of what?'

'Doesn't make sense . . . nothing makes sense.'

'Oh . . . no, make no sense.'

'You think the people who run the club know more than they're saying? Maybe Miki told the girls to keep their mouths shut?'

'Could be.' Aiko was searching through her bag for the scooter keys. 'These place with lot of foreigner working, have to be careful with police . . . could tell girls to say nothing, keep out of trouble.'

'What about this guy, you know, the *yakuza*?' Adam held up his left hand, waggling his little finger. 'D'you think they're afraid of him, protection rackets and stuff? Does that happen here?'

They turned into the street where Aiko's scooter was wait-ing, a noodle delivery bike still keeping it company. The Bar Belle's sign had been turned off and the doorway was shut up tight, the street empty and quiet, just the rubbish whis-pering as it blew about in a sudden gust of wind. One day winding down, another starting up.

'It happen, sure, but like girl say,' Aiko finally extracted the keys, 'like Oxana say, *yakuza* mostly up in Kabukicho, no down here in Roppongi.'

'What is it?'

'Kabukicho?' Aiko danced, pretending to take her clothes off, over to the scooter. 'Place for sex club and bar and soapland – you want to go now?'

Adam looked at his watch: after four; he shook his head. 'No, maybe . . .'

'I was joking, Adam!'

'Ah, Japanese jokes, my favourite – like pretending not to speak English,' he caught Aiko's arm, pulled her towards him and kissed her, 'and forcing poor tourists to have endless sex with them . . . what's a soapland anyway?'

'Where poor tourist have to *pay* to sleep with Japanese girl – want to see?'

Adam made a thing of looking at his watch again, ducking as Aiko took a playful swipe at him. 'OK, we'll do it tomorrow?'

'Tomorrow? You want to go to soapland tomorrow?'

'Yeah . . . no! I want to go to, what's it called, Kabukicho, after we've been to the hotel to settle up.' Adam eased the helmet carefully over his ears. 'See if we can find Alice.'

'That OK, I think you mean something else.'

'Trust me . . .'

Aiko sat up, pulling the sheets away from Adam. 'What happen to boyfren – Alice ol boyfren?'

'Sorry? What . . .' Adam squinted up at Aiko; he'd been doing a rapid nosedive into deep, post-sex sleep mode and had no idea what Aiko was talking about.

'Where is Alice boyfren?' Aiko switched on the table lamp next to her, lighting up Keiko's main room where they were sleeping on a pull-out futon bed that took up most of the available floor space.

'What made you remember him . . .' Adam leant over and looked at his watch on the floor, '. . . now?'

'Nobody say anything. He must be somewhere . . . could know something?'

'Steve? I suppose so. Might do.' Adam reached up and traced the line of Aiko's backbone down from her neck, watching as she stretched like a cat when he reached her coccyx. 'It was his idea to come here in the first place, maybe after he and Alice broke up he just went back travelling. Maybe he'd earned enough money and wanted to move on and Alice didn't.' Was there a pattern in any of this? If there was it was too subtle for him to spot – also way too late to start trying – and it all still left the question: where was Charlie?

'We talk tomorrow.' Aiko turned the lamp off, lay back down and snaked herself round Adam. 'You tired?'

27

A happy time on tables

The room was back the way Adam had first seen it, everything put away, everything neat, everything organised. Just no space here to be untidy in, and Aiko had insisted the job was done before they did anything else, like eat. Except, when they had finished, there was nothing in the flat that smelled anything like breakfast.

'You no hungry?' Aiko held up a bowl of the aromatic, almost fishy miso soup she was drinking. 'Sure you no want some?'

Adam shook his head. Fish soup for breakfast? He didn't think so.

'Rice?' She pointed at a bowl she'd just heated up in the microwave.

'Coffee and toast with jam? Bacon and eggs?'

'You no like Japanese *choshok* . . . breakfas?'

'Japanese *choshok* looks like supper, Aiko.'

'OK, I take you somewhere.'

'Somewhere' turned out to be the local coffee shop, part of a chain, like a kind of Japanese Starbucks, but less aggressive. Here Adam had his choice of teas, coffees, Danishes, croissants, filled rolls and sandwiches and the only downside was that just about everyone in the place was smoking. It was, he thought, the national hobby, along with talking on the mobile or texting, which a lot of people seemed to do obsessively at the same time.

Adam sat down opposite Aiko with his tray, pulled the top off the individual serving of liquid sugar, poured it in his coffee and opened the wrapping on his egg and bacon croissant. This was definitely more like it.

'Happy now, Mr Adam?'

'Oh yes.'

'We go to hotel when you finish? Check you out?'

Adam shook his head, swallowing. 'I . . . we . . . can't keep on staying at Keiko's, can we?'

'She don mind – how long for, anyway . . . when do you go home?'

With a jolt Adam was brought right back down to earth. Sitting in this nice café with Aiko wasn't reality, it was time out of line and soon, very soon, he was going to have to go home; he'd only booked the hotel room for a week, which gave him a few more nights in Tokyo. Not much time to do anything, if he stuck to his plan. He looked across the table at Aiko, feeling like she was an illusion which could disappear at any moment. He thought about his parents and about Grangie and felt bad. He thought about Charlie, that she was still missing, and felt worse. Sat here on his backside he was just wasting time, screwing everything up and achieving nothing.

'You OK, Adam?'

He stood up, took his helmet off the bench seat next to him and picked up his croissant. 'We'd better get to the hotel . . . I'll eat this on the trot.'

'We go straight up to Kabukicho, after,' Aiko picked up her

helmet and bag, following Adam out of the café. 'We find Alice, Adam, sure . . . I think this *all* about Alice.'

Adam stopped as he reached the pavement. 'D'you reckon her *yakuza* boyfriend did it? Kidnapped Charlie or something?'

Aiko shook her head. 'Don't know, Adam. We find Alice we find out.'

They sailed round the corner into the road where the New Economy Hotel was, Aiko leaning the scooter over into the right-hand turn, and drove past without stopping; a large black 4x4, a Lexus with darkened windows, was taking up all the space where they could've parked. Aiko drove on to the end of the street, took another right and found somewhere to put the scooter fifty, sixty metres down the street.

They'd walked almost back to the turn when Adam looked behind him. 'Done it again, Aiko!'

'What?'

'Your keys.'

Aiko stopped, looked at her scooter and then at Adam. 'You get keys, OK? I go talk to them at hotel first, explain,' she bowed low, 'sorry, sorry. Maybe they not charge too much.'

'OK . . . you don't mind?'

'No . . . my fault anyway. I make you stay and force you to have endless sex, right?'

Adam kissed her and walked back towards the scooter with the taste of her lipstick on his tongue, memorising the scent of her perfume, aware that he should experience every single moment, remember everything he saw, heard, touched, smelt. As he kept on forgetting to take any pictures, what was in his head was all he'd have left when this was over and he was back in London. Back in London, not walking down some street in Minowa to pick up the keys this astonishing, beautiful, extraordinary, perceptive, wicked, breathtaking girl had left behind. Again.

London. He didn't really want to think about the place and the people waiting for him there. He knew his parents were going to find out, eventually, when the credit card bill arrived, that he'd gone to Tokyo; if he returned empty-handed it was going to be a hell of a lot harder to justify what he'd done, but that was a bridge far enough away to ignore for the moment. What he was going to do about Suzy was something else. *Although*, he heard Andy say, like some little horned devil on his shoulder, *who says you have to do anything?*

He hated himself for being able to think like this, but there really was nothing to stop him from acting like nothing had happened and carrying on as before. Was there? Even though he knew there were things about his relationship with Suzy that weren't working, it wasn't like he could finish with her and be with Aiko. Just not going to happen. But having been with Aiko, even for just a few days, would he be able to compromise, pretend it'd never happened? Make do?

Pulling the keys out by their fob, Adam walked up the road again, swinging them from his finger. Heavy shit, deal with it later. He'd been mulling things over in his head on the back of the scooter and had already decided that he was going to spend the rest of his time trawling through Kabukicho until he found Alice. It was all he could do. If he hadn't found her by Monday he'd try and change his flight and go home early. There was no point in him staying any longer. And Aiko was back at her college on Monday anyway.

As he was coming up to the corner Adam heard a car start, its engine hi-revving, wheels screeching as it accelerated away. Ahead of him a black 4x4 with darkened windows squealed to a momentary halt at the junction; he noticed it had those flash-bastard, brightly chromed custom wheel trims that spun independently of the actual wheels, creating a weird optical effect that the car was moving even when it was stationary. The shadowy figure of the driver appeared to look his way, then the car turned a sharp left and sped off down the street, leaving behind a lazy vapour trail of blue exhaust. Another swift right turn at the end of the road and it was gone. The whole incident happened so quickly he hadn't had time to think about it and was fleetingly surprised when he turned the corner to go down to the hotel and saw the Lexus had gone.

Kind of wondering, in the back of his mind, why the driver had been in such a tearing hurry, Adam walked down the street, up the steps into the hotel's small foyer and into a scene of total chaos. Behind the counter two Japanese women were screeching at each other while the concierge – it looked like the man he'd met when he'd come to book a room on Thursday morning – was standing, a hand over one ear, barking down the phone. There was a European couple standing in the foyer, asking questions in broken English with what sounded like some Scandinavian accent, and as Adam came in, looking for Aiko, the concierge began pointing at him and nodding angrily.

'You the boy they want!'

The accusation stopped Adam like he'd been slapped. 'Me? Who wanted me?'

The Scandinavian man turned, frowning, puzzled. 'They took the girl. We came down . . .' he indicated the staircase with his thumb, '. . . and saw two men grab her. It was so quick.'

Adam's mouth went dry. Were they talking about Aiko? They couldn't be. He scanned left, right, then looked behind him, in case, somehow, she'd managed to go outside somehow and was coming back in again. She hadn't.

'They want *you*!' The concierge put the phone down. 'They been here two time, asking!'

'Who the hell are you *talking* about? Who's taken Aiko?'

'Bad men. Very bad men . . .'

Adam sat in the small back office of the hotel, watching the concierge talk to the two policemen who'd shown up five, ten minutes ago – he couldn't remember how long it had been. His head was like a stuck record, one thought – *AIKO HAS BEEN KIDNAPPED F'CRISSAKE – AND IT'S **ALL** MY FAULT!!* – shouting at him as it went round and round and round his brain, stopping him from thinking straight. Very bad men had been waiting for him in the hotel . . . Yoshi was a *yakuza* or Mafia or whatever, a 'bad person', so was he the one who'd taken Aiko? But why would he do that?

He saw one of the policemen turn and look through the door, look him up and down in a way that immediately made him feel guilty as hell. Guiltier. He looked away, staring at a pin board covered in notes and messages and posters, the handwritten and printed characters meaning nothing, telling no stories.

If, if, if . . . if he hadn't spotted the keys in the scooter, if Aiko hadn't suggested trying to smooth things out for him, if he hadn't let her. He'd wanted to go after Aiko (right, chase a car that had been gone for ages and in who knew what direction . . .) but had been stopped by the concierge, made to stay and wait until the police arrived. And a lot of good they seemed to be doing. And now here he was, surrounded by people who didn't speak much or anything of his language, didn't trust him, didn't look like they were *doing* anything!

'What the girl name?'

Adam looked round to find the concierge had come into the office. 'Aiko . . . she's called Aiko.'

'Family name, you give me family name?'

Family name? He'd never asked, never thought to. He shook his head. 'Sorry, don't know.'

The concierge said something to the police over his shoulder, listening to their reply. 'How long you know?'

'Um . . . not long . . . about two days.'

The man nodded – Adam couldn't read his expression at all – and went out of the room, leaving him alone again. What did he know about Aiko? Since they'd met they'd hardly been out of each other's sight, spent hours in bed, not many of them actually asleep; emotionally he knew her, he could describe her, physically, in minute detail, but what was her name, where did she live, what was her mobile number? Not a chance. He could be no help at all.

A feeling of total hopelessness fell on him like a slow-motion blanket of fog, draining his ability to be positive, making him want to cry tears of rage and frustration, paralysing him. A memory opened, blossoming in his head: sitting with Suzy in the café, the enthusiasm he'd felt pumping him up, creating an aura of such optimism that he could actually do something and make a difference. And now, in this poky room in a hotel in Tokyo, the dream was dust. Not only had he not found Charlie, he'd also lost Aiko. How crap was that?

Adam heard a door open, letting in outside noises, and

then voices; he moved so more of the small foyer came into view and saw three more people had arrived, two more Japanese wearing suits – plain-clothes cops? – and a European. Who was he? The European man glanced at Adam, frowning, the way you do when you realise you're being watched, leant across to one of the plain-clothes newcomers and then walked into the room.

'Adam Grey?'

It was Adam's turn to looked perplexed, and he just nodded.

'I'm with the embassy.' The man, youngish – Adam thought probably mid-twenties, smart, at ease and with that couldn't-give-a-toss manner he assumed came from breeding and a private education – put out his hand. 'Simon Palmer.'

Adam shook his hand quickly and let go. 'How d'you know my name?'

'You told the hotel when you booked the room, remember? Nothing suspicious.' Simon sat on the edge of the desk that took up most of the floor space in the office. 'When the concierge called the police about the abduction, he also told them about the men who'd been coming here asking about you. Your name rang alarm bells because you've been reported as missing by your parents.'

28

Credulity that remark

Adam was stunned. His parents knew he was in Tokyo? Since when?

Simon Palmer supplied the answer without the question being asked. 'Interpol sent the information through a couple of days ago.'

'*Inter*pol? What am I, some kind of gangster on the run?'

'Just the way things happen, Adam; protocol . . . it's what makes the world go round.'

Adam wasn't really listening, still trying to work out how his parents had found out he was in Japan. Had Suzy dumped him in it? Unlikely. It was always possible the credit card bill had arrived earlier than he thought it would. More than likely. Could Alice have made another phone call and said she'd seen him? He was beginning to wonder if he actually had seen her in that Roppongi back street, or whether it had just been someone who looked like her.

Thinking about Alice brought Charlie into sharp focus, the events of the previous half hour or so having pushed her to the back of his mind. 'My sister . . . have they found my sister?'

'Charlotte? No, I'm afraid not as yet.' Palmer stood up. 'The police –'

'She didn't leave that club with anyone, you know. Alice was lying.'

'Sorry?'

'My sister never left the Bar Belle with any Japanese bloke . . . if she's been kidnapped by anyone it's going to be Alice's boyfriend, the *yakuza* type.'

'Did you realise that the people who took your friend were, how shall I put it, of the same "type"?'

Adam nodded. 'We phoned the hotel last night,' he pointed out of the door. 'it must've been that guy who told Aiko about them.'

'And you still came here?'

'*We* didn't know they were camped outside, and anyway, what would some Japanese crim want with me? Or Aiko?'

'As I was about to say a moment ago, the police want you to go back to their station with them . . .'

'What for? I don't *know* anything, I didn't *see* anything – I wasn't here when it happened, right, otherwise they'd've taken me, wouldn't they? Like, doh?'

'It's OK, Adam, I understand that you're upset, but there are formalities.' Palmer was making 'calm down' signals with his hands as he spoke quietly but firmly. 'At the moment the police have no idea who has been kidnapped – as, apparently, you only know the young woman's first name – and they have no idea why or by whom. They need all the help they can get, and you are one of the people who can and must give it to them, OK?'

'Yeah, OK . . . sure. Sorry, I'm a bit –'

'I do understand; I'll come with you to the station – they have interpreters there. Then I'll come back later to pick you up and take you to the hotel where your parents will be staying when they arrive on Monday.'

199

'My *what*?'

They fly out tomorrow, the 9.oo a.m. flight.'

'My *parents* are coming to Tokyo?'

'That's what my colleague in the F and C told me.'

'Effencee?'

'Foreign and Commonwealth office. They passed the message on.'

'Jeee-zus . . .'

'Adventure over, I suppose.'

'You condescending bastard.' Adam's lip curled. 'You think I came all the way over here for a stupid *adventure*? My sister's missing, she could be *dead* for all *anyone* seems to care, and *I* came out here to find her because fucking *nothing* was happening and no one was doing anything. I did *not* come over here for some crap bloody adventure, OK?'

Palmer physically backed off. 'I think you'll find that quite a lot has been going on –'

'And I think *you'll* find that whatever whoever has been doing, it hasn't achieved much. Charlie's still missing, and that's all that counts.'

'Look,' Palmer glanced over his shoulder at the waiting policemen, 'I realise you've been through a lot, and that that was a slightly insensitive remark – for which I apologise – but can we move on, please? The quicker we get you cooperating with the police here, the quicker your friend'll be found. And I'll make some more enquiries about your sister.'

Adam sat on one of a line of interconnected plastic seats in the cold, sterile light cast by banks of fluorescent strips set into the ceiling, the kind of light that illuminated but made people look recently dead. He'd been brought out here, to this bland, characterless corridor in the police station by one of the interpreters; he was supposed to wait for the Simon Palmer bloke to pick him up and take him to the hotel where he was going to have to phone his parents. And wouldn't *that* be an interesting conversation.

What was he going to say? *'Don't bother coming over, I've got it all under control'*? Hardly. And what were they going to say to him? He didn't want to think about it; instead, he got up and stretched, wondering how the police were getting on with the Scandinavian couple and the staff from the New Economy. He'd been completely useless, a total waste of space. He knew nothing about Aiko, no addresses where they'd stayed, either with Kenichi and Ayumi or Keiko, no phone numbers, no last names. Even Alice's *yakuza* boyfriend was only probably called 'Yoshi'. It was a joke, and under any other circumstances it would've made him laugh, but not now.

Simon Palmer looked at his watch, a brand-new Seiko Arctura he'd bought duty-free down in Akihabara the week before; the sleek, brushed stainless-steel case and strap glinted in the afternoon sun that was streaming through his office window, reminding him there were some perks to being a put-upon very junior member of the embassy staff. Three thirty, time to go back to the police station and get the boy, Adam Grey. Mouthy little bastard, going off on one at him at that backpacker hotel. Except, if his sister had gone missing, he supposed he'd want something done about it, and, he had to admit, from what little he knew not a lot had been done so far.

Why these girls came here and worked in the hostess bars in the first place was beyond him, and while he certainly didn't think they deserved what they got, it wasn't as if they didn't know what was what. Surely. Palmer got up and then sat straight back down again, remembering that he was going to phone the boy's parents, let them know their son was safe. He checked his watch, a little after three thirty now, about 7:35 a.m. GMT, and a pretty good time to call. He picked up the handset, punched an outside line and then the line of digits written on the pad in front of him. There was a click and then the familiar UK ring tone. Three, four rings later the call was picked up and he heard a drowsy voice answer with the phone number.

'Mr Grey?'

'Yes?'

'My name's Simon Palmer, from the embassy in Tokyo?'

'Oh, right . . .' The voice instantly lost its sleepy cadence and Simon heard another, female, voice ask who was there. 'The embassy . . . Tokyo . . . is this something to do with Charlie, Mr, um, Parker?'

'Palmer. No . . . no, I'm afraid not, Mr Grey.'

'Oh . . .'

'But it is some good news. We've found Adam and he's safe and well. He'll be waiting for you at the hotel when you arrive on Monday.'

'Is he with you now – can we speak to him?' Palmer heard Mr Grey say *they've found Adam* to the other person, presumably his wife.

'I'm just going to pick him up now, Mr Grey, and as soon as he's at the hotel, I'll get him to call you.'

'You say he's OK – d'you know where he's been at all, what he's been up to?'

'I don't know any of the details, Mr Grey. I'm sorry.' Palmer thought that now was probably not the time to explain to

Mr Grey that in the few days his son had been in Tokyo he'd somehow managed to get himself mixed up with the kidnapping of a young woman by the local bad guys. Not part of his remit.

'OK . . . OK . . . when d'you think he'll call?'

'Oh,' Palmer glanced at his watch again, 'I'd say in about an hour.'

All Adam could do now was mooch around, wait and worry about Aiko and what Yoshi was doing; it had to be Yoshi . . . who else could it be? What had happened to her was all his fault, he should never have got her involved. But then how was *he* to know . . . he stopped pacing up and down, driving himself nuts with what he *should* have done and started trying to think what he *could* be doing.

He walked over to his jacket, which was lying in a crumpled heap where he'd thrown it on to one of the chairs. Picking it up he started feeling it to see if there was some chewing gum in any of the pockets; you never knew. Three pockets came up empty, just fluff, and then . . . he pulled out a cartoon character fob. Attached to the key to Aiko's scooter.

The scooter was still parked round the corner from the hotel, with the two helmets, one in the top box, the other under the seat. Really shouldn't be left there, should it . . . Could he? Could he just up and go off on Aiko's scooter to search for Alice in Kabukicho, like he'd planned? He looked round. No one to stop him. And the longer he waited the more chance of Mr Embassy appearing to take him off some place or other, probably miles away from anywhere he wanted to be. This police station hadn't taken long to get to and he was sure he'd seen a subway entrance at the bottom of the street they'd turned into to get here. Adam looked at the key in the palm of his hand. It was either stay here and do nothing useful, or get off his arse and at least *try*. He stood up. Mad idea, but what the hell . . .

It had been a crazed journey. Insanity. On top of never having actually ridden a scooter as anything but a passenger, he was in a city he didn't know and using a tourist map that lacked detail, to put it mildly. He'd only the vaguest notion of where he was going, able only to work out that if he went down this one street until he came to a junction and turned right, he would, eventually and with more than a little luck, end up somewhere near where he wanted to be. The biggest of all the many flaws in his plan was his lack of experience on two wheels. He'd been meaning to get his act together and take his CBT, but other stuff kept on getting in the way. And then there was the fact that he didn't *actually* own a scooter.

An hour after setting out from Minowa, a red light stopped Adam at a major junction and, looking at the map, he realised the cross street was the Meiji-dori and that his destination was, finally, only a few hundred metres down the road. It was now five o'clock, he was starving hungry and wondering why the hell he hadn't simply taken the subway; just because you had a key didn't mean you had to use it. He really should try and remember that in future.

He eventually found somewhere to park the scooter, locked up his helmet and looked across the wide street at the blitz of neon, behind which the guidebook said lay a maze of low rent bars, clubs and restaurants, with 'a good chance of spotting members of the *yakuza* crime syndicates'. Which was all very picturesque, but what he really needed was a good chance of cornering a certain Alice Reardon. He walked down to the nearest set of lights and waited until they turned red.

29

Let's spend the shining moment on the street

'He's not here?' Simon Palmer frowned, momentarily non-plussed. 'What d'you mean "not here"? Where's he gone? He's supposed to be here so I can pick him up and take him to a hotel.'

It was hard to tell if the plain-clothes officer, one of the two he'd gone to the hotel with to pick up Adam Grey, was embarrassed, couldn't care less or had no opinion at all about the disappearance of the boy. He could be really torn up about it, for all Palmer knew, because his face never changed. Not a twitch.

'Aporogy.' The officer bowed. 'No person see him walk away. Very aporogy.'

Great! He'd just walked out of the front door! Palmer could feel the tension dragging its sharp, heated knife blades across his shoulders. He was supposed to be driving the bloody boy to the hotel and getting him to call his parents in, he checked, thirty-five *sodding* minutes. Except the *bloody* boy wasn't here, he was out there, somewhere, in this ridiculously huge city of twenty-seven million people.

'Do you have his description?'

'Description? Yes.' The policeman brought a notepad out

of his pocket and started flicking through pages.

'No . . . no, I don't want – look will you put out an APB, or whatever you call it here, to all your stations? Get people looking for him?'

'Moment prease. I come someone better Engrish.' The officer turned and left Palmer waiting by the front desk. There were days when you wished you'd never woken up and this was very definitely one of those.

It was the smell that drew Adam. Kebabs. It was definitely kebabs. And when he turned the corner he saw a big red van, its side down and with two big lumps of doner spinning slowly like torture victims on their vertical spits. Memories of drunken trawls with his mates through the West End, where a greasy doner, topped with evil chilli sauce, was the obligatory finale, came flooding back.

As homesick as he was hungry, Adam bought a chicken doner wrap and stood near the van as he ate it, half watching the passing street traffic, half trying to work out what the hell he thought he was doing. He should be in some hotel now, having had his ear chewed off by irate, mega-pissed off parents; instead he was about to start wandering round what looked like Soho on steroids – layer upon layer of strip joints, dive bars and clubs, all touting for business from lurid street-to-sky towers of signs, all with offers of girls and booze and an escape from reality. It was all a sham, like him. Maybe he should do everyone a favour and give up any more stupid attempts to find Aiko, Alice, Yoshi or Charlie. Cos who was he kidding . . . what chance did he have in a place like this?

He stood, eating his way through the wrap, hardly aware of the taste, just putting fuel into the engine; this time in a few days he'd be back in London – in just over a *week*, fer-crissake, he be back at college! – and Tokyo would all be over, for him. A dubious act of rank stupidity he'd be able to look back on for the rest of his life. Oh joy.

Still, he did have choices. He could phone the embassy, apologise to that Palmer bloke and arrange to go to the hotel. Or . . . ? Well, he could do what he'd come here to Kabukicho to do, which was give it one last go, and *then* call the embassy. Adam finished the doner. In London he'd probably have screwed up the paper and dropped it; here in Tokyo there were rubbish bins everywhere, he'd even noticed recycling points built into some of the vending machines, and the streets were clean. He looked for a bin, used it – when in Japan, etc. – and wiped his hands on his jeans. If he was going to get anywhere, he'd better make a move.

As he walked past the ground-floor Penthouse Gentlemen's Club, past the stairway down to the Carol House, the sign for the Ritz Club and the electric pink back-ground with a life-size naked blonde (much too like Charlie for comfort) advertising the Broadway Gentlemen's Club, it occurred to him that maybe working in 'fancy dress' in some bar in Roppongi wasn't such a bad deal. Better than being here.

So many thoughts were jumping to the front of his head Adam was finding it hard to concentrate on one for more than a few seconds . . . Aiko was probably here, in some basement room or six floors up where he'd never find her – and never put a last name to her first. How were the police ever going to discover her whereabouts – tell her parents – without *that* information? Adam stopped next to a sign that told him Lady Club Bugsy was five floors up above him, should he wish to visit. Another thought had just occurred . . . the only person he knew who knew all about Aiko, *and* the only person whose address he had more than a vague idea about, was Keiko. He looked at his watch. She'd still be working, probably wouldn't get back to her apartment for another hour or two, so no point trying to get there yet.

He'd carry on searching and then take another nerve-wracking scooter ride. This time he'd kind of know where he was going as Aiko had marked the approximate place where Keiko lived on his map when she'd been showing him the route they'd taken the night before. What would this scuzball Yoshi do when he found Aiko didn't know anything about him – if he believed her? Beat her up, then throw her out? Worse? Adam felt his stomach clench at the thought of how bad worse could be.

Pushing the unwanted images and scenarios out of his head, he carried on walking, concentrating on looking for any signs of Alice or sightings of men with their little fingers cut off. He had a fair idea of what he'd do if he saw Alice, but no notion of what might happen if he bumped into some actual neighbourhood *yakuza*. The guidebook said they had big hair and flashy, retro suits, so they were obviously quite upfront about who they were and what they did and hopefully wouldn't be too difficult to spot.

With no idea of where he was going, no plan, like when he'd quartered the map of Roppongi, Adam just walked. And walked and walked. He went down little streets crowded with bars, some decorated like log cabins, others like miniature medieval castles, one place coming complete with a 'Welcome' mat outside it. He passed flashy neon-lit hotels and wandered down streets which were completely made up of micro-restaurants, often just simple benches at a stall, others only doing take-away. At most of these places the food was being cooked on charcoal right in front of you and the air was filled with smells of grilled squid and king prawns. But no sign anywhere of Alice.

It was still light, but the sun was going down, more neon going on and the human traffic in the streets was picking up as the evening's punters began to arrive. He came to a crossroads and opposite him he saw a familiar sign amongst the alien mass of adverts and shop fronts: Häagen-Dazs. He joined the small queue and bought a double-scoop cone of mint-chocolate chip and pistachio. Another reminder of home and nights out with Suzy at the flicks. He was cursing his memory bank for reminding him of one more thing he had piled up to deal with, when he thought he saw a dark-haired European girl, wearing a red top, in the kind of amusement arcade place across the road.

The girl – could he be lucky enough for it to be Alice? – moved out of his line of sight and he sprinted across the road and in through open doors of the arcade. The noise inside was extreme – not the chaos of electronic gunfire, space attack and road rage, like in London arcades, but the shattering din of hundreds and thousands of humungous ball bearings being poured continuously from the ceiling, down chutes and into ranks of machines. It was like being physically assaulted by sound and for a moment Adam couldn't think what he was supposed to be doing, then he remembered. The girl.

He jogged along the narrow corridor running the length of the arcade, checking down each of the rows of back-to-back machines. Almost all of them had someone playing, usually smoking as they fed in coins and watched the steel balls dance around the flashing screen. Mesmerised. No one paid him the slightest attention as he scanned the aisles for a sign of the girl he'd seen. About two thirds of the way down he was sure he'd just missed her as a flash of red disappeared at the end of the row he was passing.

Adam hesitated – go down this row, or jump to the next and run down that one? A second later he was pelting down the next aisle. Getting to the end of it, and skidding round the corner on the shiny lino floor, he almost collided with a middle-aged man carrying a basket packed full of ball bearings. The man staggered backwards out of his way, spilling some of the shiny steel spheres, which skittered away like small globules of mercury. Stop and help him pick them up? Adam glanced the way he presumed the girl had gone and saw that flash of red again. Not today. He ran, ignoring the angry voice behind him.

The girl had turned a corner and as Adam got to it he saw her exiting the arcade on to another street. As she went out she turned and looked back, straight through him. Not Alice. Nothing like her. Adam, deflated, went from running full pelt to a stumbling halt, and watched whoever it was walk away; then he heard, through the racket, raised voices behind him and jogged quickly out of the place before any of the trouble he'd caused could catch up with him.

Back out on the street, the sky visibly darkening, electric lights, fluorescents and strobes were now vying for attention, casting mysterious shadows and changing the world around him. No Alice, no sign so far of anyone remotely fitting the description of a *yakuza*, no real point in being here much longer. Up ahead, looking totally surreal, Adam saw a girl dressed as a bride – veil, off-the-shoulder satin and lace dress, white, elbow-length gloves, the lot – standing outside a building handing out flyers; something told him they weren't advertising a sale at a nearby wedding shop.

As he walked past her he couldn't help smiling as he waved 'no' when the girl offered him a flyer. She looked pretty and ridiculous at the same time. Adam glanced at his watch: coming up to seven o'clock. He should be making tracks back to where he'd parked the scooter so he could try and get in touch with Keiko. OK, problem No. 1 – where was he? He got out his guidebook, turned back and walked up to the bride.

'Scuse me?'

'*Hai?*'

Adam pointed to the map in his hand. '*Yasukuni-dori?*'

'*Sou desu . . .*' The girl nodded, speaking some more as she pointed up the road, holding up two fingers and then indicating a right turn. '*Oké?*'

'OK, thanks,' Adam bowed, grinning.

'No probrem!'

'Bye . . .'

'*Dewa mata.*'

Adam walked up the road, thinking that actually the 'bride' was really quite cute. He went past the first turning, and as he was about to take the next one he saw a big black 4x4 with darkened windows parked a few metres away on the opposite side of the street. He only noticed it because of the lights glinting off its shiny, chromed custom 'spinning rim' wheel trim. The car must just recently have been parked as they were still swinging round and round, producing that strange illusion of forward motion. It was a Lexus.

'Shit, shit, shit!'

'What's up, Si?'

Palmer looked up to see Chris Taylor, the other junior aide with whom he shared the tiny office, standing at the door. 'What're you doing here, Chris – thought you were off today?'

'Left my phone charger behind. What's the problem?'

'They found that kid who'd been reported missing, and I had to go and pick him up.'

'The brother of the girl . . .' Taylor snapped his fingers, '. . . Charlotte Grey?'

'The same.'

'Oh . . . so why the meltdown?'

'I left him at the police station, couldn't see much point in my wasting my *entire* day hanging round there. Told him I'd come back and pick him up after he'd "assisted the police with their enquires".'

'Seems reasonable.'

'Except he wasn't there when I went back. Pissed off somewhere, again.'

'He'll turn up.'

'I've already called the parents and told them he'll be phoning them from the hotel.'

'Ah . . . shit, shit, shit.'

'Exactly.'

30

Modal shift

Adam gawped at the black 4x4, confused, and looked up and then down the street, back the way he'd come. The bride saw him, caught his eye and waved. And that broke the spell. He couldn't stand around like a total dummy, staring at some car. He stuck out here enough, being European, without making a thing of it. He turned down the street the girl had told him to take and stopped, staring back at the car.

Could it be the same one he'd seen outside the New Economy Hotel? Yoshi's Lexus? What were the chances of there being another one *exactly* like it, black windows, fancy wheel trim and all? For all he knew they were standard-issue *yakuza* vehicles, but this was the first one he'd noticed and it was parked in the right kind of area.

He'd been hoping, if he was lucky, to catch sight of a person, someone he could maybe follow or confront. What should he do now that he might, possibly, have found a person's car instead? It didn't take a genius to work out that the only thing he could do was stake it out and hope he saw where the person who drove it away had come from. And hope Aiko was there, right? Crap plan. Especially as there wasn't really anywhere that he could hang around and watch without being seen.

But why the *hell* was he trying to hide? Why, exactly?

When you were on your own, with no one else to run ideas by, no one to talk things over with and see stuff from another point of view, it was so easy to lead yourself up the garden path. Surely what he wanted was for Yoshi to see him hanging round his car, to make the connection that this *gaijin* eyeing up his wheels was the same one he'd been trying to find? Adam felt like nutting the wall he was standing next to, could hear the fat bespectacled old geezer in army uniform, from some sitcom his parents liked to watch on vid, saying *'Stupid boy!'*.

Before he could do anything about making himself ultra visible, Adam saw a door open in the building behind the Lexus and two men – longish, slicked-back hair, dark suits, white shirts – come out, get straight into the car and drive away, leaving him staring at nothing but an empty parking space. This could not have happened! He felt like a small child who'd just been offered a gift, only to have it rudely snatched away before he could even touch it. He wanted to scream, *'It's not FAIR!'*, but what good would that do?

He walked over to look at the door the men had come out of; nondescript, scuffed, grey-painted, lacking a handle and with greasy finger marks where people pushed to get in, it held no clues as to what or who was behind it. Adam shoved, just in case, though if it'd been open he had no idea what he'd have done next. Stepping back he looked at the entryphone: no label – even in Japanese – and a single button. Just the one business being run from behind it, then. He could push the buzzer and see what happened, but if someone answered it was going to be in a language he couldn't understand or speak, so there wasn't much point. Was there?

Adam, poised, ready to run, like when he and Andy had used to play Knock Down Ginger when they were kids, reached out and pressed the buzzer. I mean, he thought, why the hell not?

Nothing happened.

Having gone this far he pressed it again, harder and longer this time, in case the connection was bad. And waited. Then stood back to look up and see if there were any lights on in the floors above . . . none he could see. And waited.

Click . . . hum . . . zzz

'Hai?'

Japanese for 'yes' – he'd picked up that much since he'd arrived – but not spoken by someone from Japan . . . a voice he recognised . . . a woman, girl . . .

'Donata des ka?'

Jeezus! 'Alice?'

'Oh shit . . .'

'Alice, let me in, it's Adam!'

'I know . . .' Alice's voice, fuzzed-up by the cheap loudspeaker, sounded tired and tense at the same time. 'What the *hell* are you doing here?'

'Are you alone? Let me in, I've gotta talk to you!'

'Go away.'

Adam kicked the door, which achieved nothing except to send a jarring pain up his leg. 'BLOODY LET ME IN, ALICE!'

'Go away, Adam, just piss off . . . there'll just be more trouble if you don't.'

Adam, tensed and getting a small hit of adrenaline, glanced around. A couple of people were looking his way but no one seemed like they were about to get involved.

'I'm staying right here until you open the door, Alice . . . honest.'

Empty noise, the sound of nothing.

'Alice?'

Electric hush, but one that was finally broken by the *clunk-buzz* of the lock being opened. Adam pushed the door – it was heavier that it looked – and walked into a short, narrow corridor that led to a flight of stairs. Behind him the door swung shut with a metallic thud and he looked over his shoulder to see that the back of it was reinforced with steel bars and big, locking bolts. Some serious security here.

He started up the stairs, the smell of cooking and stale sweat and cigarettes tainting the sour air. At the first landing there were two doors, both closed. Adam stopped and listened for some sound, some evidence of occupation, but there was nothing. He went round to the next staircase and looked up; he took a couple of involuntary steps backwards when he saw someone, a girl, on the next landing looking back down at him. The single low-wattage light bulb hanging from the ceiling partially silhouetted her against the off-white wall, but he realised it was Alice and that this time she didn't have anywhere to run.

'Howd'you find me, Adam?'

'Luck . . . how did they know where to find me, though? No one knew I was supposed to be at that hotel.'

'Dunno . . . must've told someone Yoshi knows.' Alice looked away, pushing her hair back over her ears.

'Don't think so . . .'

'You told Miki.'

'Miki?'

'At the Bar Belle?' Alice's mouth twitched in a fake smile.

Adam stopped, one foot on a stair; Miki'd known a hell of lot more than she'd let on, but no surprises there. 'Shall I, um, come up?'

Alice sniffed and nodded, turning away. 'You shouldn't be here, Adam . . . you *really* shouldn't.'

'I came to find Charlie, Alice.' Adam reached the second landing and saw Alice had gone into a room off it. 'Where is she?'

Alice flinched, the question making her react as if she'd been threatened, turning away from Adam, hugging herself. He walked though the doorway into what was obviously an office – high-backed leather chair behind a mid-sized, glass-topped desk, the desk littered with papers, old food containers, a couple of glasses and a phone.

'Where is she, Alice? I know she didn't leave the Bar Belle with anyone, that she'd gone days before . . . you made all that up, right?' Adam reached out to try and get Alice to look at him. 'Why, Alice? Why d'you do that?'

Alice refused to budge. 'None of your business.'

'What the hell d'you mean? She's my *sister*, fercrissake, why wouldn't it be my business?' Adam grabbed Alice by the shoulders and dragged her round to face him. 'My parents think she's *dead*, Alice!'

She looked up at him, eyes narrowed, lips pursed. 'Good.'

Good? Adam jerked back like she'd spat at him, shocked by what she'd said, almost more than by the way she looked back at him. In the unforgiving tungsten light she was still pretty, but her expression was cold, almost hateful; she glanced at him, her heavily mascaraed eyes like dark, cynical smudges, pinhole pupils in her pale blue irises. 'What's happened to you?'

Alice moved away, back nearer the desk. 'Nothing. I'm fine

218

. . . totally.' She glanced down, absentmindedly clearing empty food containers off the glass top and dropping them into a waste bin. 'Why're you here?'

'I told you, I came to find Charlie.'

'I mean why're you *here*?' Alice tapped the glass desktop with a long French-polished nail.

'I came looking for you, Alice, and for Aiko. I know she was kidnapped by your friend Yoshi.'

'Who's a clever little detective!' Alice's smile morphed slowly into a sneer. 'Why should I tell you *any*thing?'

'Why?' Adam's temper volcanoed. 'I'll tell you fucking *why*, you bitch!' He lunged across the room, forcing Alice backwards against the table, which knocked the phone on to the floor. 'Because if you don't I'll kick the living shit out of you, OK?'

In the silence Adam could hear his heart beating, and in the background the dialling tone of the phone that had been tipped off the desk. Would he really hit Alice? God, he hoped he'd never have to find out . . .

'Don't think I don't mean it, Alice.'

'You call *me* a bitch! Your slut sister took my boyfriend, screwed him behind my back and just *took* him – she knew I loved him, she knew, but what bloody *Charlie* wants, bloody *Charlie* gets, right? Spoilt brat . . .'

'This is all about some bloke?' Adam found himself in one of those this-does-not-compute situations. 'You started all this because your *boyfriend* left you for Charlie? Are you deranged, or what?'

Alice picked up a glass from the desk and threw it in Adam's direction; it sailed past his left shoulder and shattered against the wall. 'Steve did *not* leave me, bastard – *she* bloody *stole* him! OK!' Shouting, irate . . . and then a smaller voice, but still hard. 'Steve wouldn't leave me. He wouldn't . . .'

Adam stood observing Alice, the 'now' Alice who was so different from the 'then' version he'd last seen the day before she and Charlie had left to go on their trip. Could this whole thing be about some bloke from Brighton? Surely . . .

'You telling me this really is all down to Steve? Crissake, Alice!'

'She took him, you little shit – what d'you know about anything, anyway?'

He stared at Alice's eyes, now unable to meet his, and a penny dropped. 'He found out you were fooling round on the side with Yoshi, didn't he . . . you met Yoshi at the club and had a thing happening . . . I bet that was it, right? *You* were the one playing away from home, and *that's* why Stevie-boy upped and left. Charlie's your friend, Alice, I know she wouldn't do anything behind your back.' Adam looked round the room. 'What's so attractive about this side of the fence, Alice? What's Yoshi got going for him . . . he's got the drug-dealer motor and the sidekicks . . .'

'Piss off!' Another glass flew his way, this one making Adam duck. 'You don't know a bloody thing, so just piss off out of here and leave me alone!'

'Tell me where she is!'

'*I* don't bloody know, do I – how should *I* know? They did-n't leave a note, I haven't had a *postcard* . . .' Alice picked up a random piece of paper off the desk and pretended to read it. '"Having a lovely time screwing your boyfriend, wish you were here, love Charlie 'n' Steve" – and know what? I don't fucking *care* where they are. I hope she is dead . . .'

'Alice . . . Alice that's such a *crap* thing to say!'

'Yeah . . .' Adam saw tears start to stream down Alice's cheeks, dragging tiny, jagged rivulets of black mascara over her face, '. . . yeah, it is . . . but it was a *shitty, shitty* thing to do, OK?'

'OK, if you say so . . .'

Alice looked like she was coming apart at the seams, like the story she'd made up about Charlie, and Adam wondered what would happen if he pushed too far. But there were things he had to know.

'What happened, Alice?'

'I went back to the flat a couple of weeks ago . . .' Alice sniffed hard and stood up straighter. 'I went back and they'd gone, packed up and moved out.'

'When did they leave? When you called my parents?'

Alice shrugged. 'Before.'

'Why'd you do that . . . why make all that shit up?'

'She screwed me over.'

'So pretending she'd been kidnapped was your way of getting your own back, right?' Adam saw Alice look smugly back at him. 'What else are you lining up and snorting, Alice? Just how fried *is* your brain – have you *any* idea how much crap you've stirred up?'

'Why should I care.'

A statement, not a question; Adam shook his head. 'All this over some piss-stupid boyfriend . . . I can't bloody believe it! What about Aiko – why'd they take her? Why was this guy Yoshi so interested in me anyway?'

'He . . .' Alice wiped her nose across the back of her hand, blinking the last of the tears out of her eyes. 'He's like protective, OK? He wanted to tell you to *leave me alone*! Yoshi likes to keep me happy.'

Adam looked away; yeah, right. 'Why'd you freak like that

when you saw me?'

'Last person I expected to see . . . didn't think anyone'd come *looking* for her.'

'She was missing, Alice, what'd you *think* was going to happen?'

'She not bloody missing, is she! She's out there, with Steve . . . thought you'd get an email or something.'

'Well we didn't.' Adam was finding it hard to take in that everything – every bloody thing – that had happened over the last two weeks was all down to this strung-out girl on the revenge mission from hell. 'If this bloke of yours, this Yoshi, if he wanted me, why take her? Why take Aiko, she doesn't *know* anything?'

'She knew you . . . the boys Yoshi had sent over there aren't the brightest bulbs in the box, OK? They were bored, you hadn't shown, so they took the next best thing, someone who said they were your friend.' Alice almost smiled. 'Yoshi blew a major fuse when they got back here with her, went totally rabid on them.'

'Jeezus!' Adam could feel panic and frustration rising up inside him, feeding on each other. 'What's happened to her . . . did he do anything to her, Alice? Where the hell is she?'

'Yoshi do nuffin you *gáru-frendo*.'

Adam swung round to find a man standing behind him on the landing; a slight figure, shorter than him by a couple of inches, the light picking out the craters on his badly pock-marked face and reflecting dully off what looked like a very expensive black silk suit. The man sniffed and nodded at him, staring through the blank, solid lenses of a pair of Oakleys. Adam's mouth went dry.

31

Have a nice day penguin duck

Yoshi walked into the room, making for his desk. As he went past Adam his left arm snaked upwards like a whip and the back of his hand whacked Adam's face with a noise like a Christmas cracker being pulled. It all happened so quickly, so stunningly, painfully fast, that Yoshi was picking the phone up off the floor and sitting down in his chair before Adam – dazed, his cheek burning, tiny coloured lights flashing in front of his eyes – could work out what had happened.

Rubbing his chin and pushing with his tongue to test if any teeth had come loose, he realised he'd been so zeroed in on Alice he hadn't heard anyone coming up the stairs; and if Yoshi was here it more than likely meant there were others as well.

Adam shook his head; Alice had gone behind the desk and was standing close by Yoshi, who was leaning forward, elbows in front of him, his hands steepled, a fair sized diamond ring on his left hand sparkling with a subdued white fire. No wonder his face hurt. Adam could see that the little finger of Yoshi's left hand had the first joint missing and found himself wondering why, at the same time knowing now wasn't the time to ask.

'I think that was Yoshi's way of saying goodbye, Adam.'

Adam ignored her and looked directly at Yoshi's sunglasses. 'Where's Aiko?'

'He threw her out. She's gone, OK? Not here.'

'I wasn't talking to you.' The shock of having been slapped, like a naughty child, had turned to anger and Adam could feel himself about to lose it. But as his fists bunched he saw Yoshi reach into his jacket, slowly. And equally slowly put a black pistol down on the desk in front of him, where it lay like a silent, terminal threat.

Adam watched him, this small, neat, violent man, his nails shining, his expensive jewellery and elegant suit, cut so that his gun wouldn't show . . . watched him like you'd watch some feral creature who was probably about to attack you. Mindful that it was built to kill, and you weren't.

He was *so* out of his depth.

'We work together.' Alice put a hand on the back of the leather chair. 'I'm part of the team now . . .' She leant down and said something in heavily accented Japanese to Yoshi, who nodded and lit a cigarette. 'Yoshi's going places, taking me with him.'

'What happened to you, Alice? When did you completely lose the plot?'

'Screw you.'

'*Scaru-yu!*' Yoshi laughed a slightly high-pitched giggle, spun the pistol round with his finger, picked it up and pointed it at Adam. Rock steady, no shaking. He could see the graceful spiral of the barrel's rifling disappearing down towards the bullet he knew must be waiting in the chamber. Behind the gun Adam was aware of Yoshi's amused smile, gold glinting in his mouth.

The *yakuza* got up from his chair and came out in front of

the desk, gun still pointing directly at Adam. He walked up to him and jabbed the barrel, like a punch, into his stomach. Adam, already tensed up, took the blow and just managed not to be winded by it, staggering a couple of steps backwards and clutching his stomach. '*Gooda-bi. Oké?*'

Alice looked almost proud. 'I'm teaching him English.'

'Right . . . yeah . . . course you are.' Adam stood his ground, his stomach muscles really hurting. 'He's, um, he's very good.'

Alice ran her tongue backwards and forwards over her top gum and said something in Japanese to Yoshi, who nodded, grinned, then blanked his face as he whipped the gun up at Adam's face and pulled back the hammer. This time the barrel was shaking slightly. 'He thinks you're taking the piss, Adam.'

'I can tell.'

'He doesn't like that.'

'Tell him I'm not.'

'Say sorry, Adam . . .'

'Why're you doing this?'

'Cos I can. Say sorry.'

Adam could tell that for Alice this was payback time; he looked straight at Yoshi. 'I'm sorry.'

'Bye, Adam.'

'So I just go?'

'Unless you want another slapping, yeah . . . yeah, I would.'

'OK.' Adam made to leave, then stopped. 'What should I tell your parents?'

'Sod off, Adam.'

As he moved – slowly, even though he wanted so much to run – Adam heard a loud, oiled, metallic click. The sound of a firing pin meeting air, not a waiting percussion cap. No bullet in the barrel. He turned and saw Yoshi was nodding and smiling, the pistol still pointed directly at him. '*Beng-beng . . . ha-ha!*'

'Is that Simon Palmer?'

'Jesus, where the *hell* have you been?'

'Kabukicho.' Adam, leaning against the phone booth, watched the early night-time traffic stop-start along the Yasukuni-dori; he was tired and wired, kind of wouldn't mind getting to a bog as he really had nearly crapped himself back in that office.

'What on earth did you go there for?'

'I was looking for Aiko.'

'Did you find her?'

'No, but she's free, they let her go.'

'Where are you now?'

'On the main drag, the Yasu-whatsit.'

'Whereabouts?'

Adam glanced round for some kind of landmark. 'Near a big cinema . . .'

'Stay there, I'll come and get you.'

'But –' The dialling tone buzzed in his ear. Adam replaced the handset.

All around him coloured lights rose and fell across the faces of the buildings on either side of the wide main road; they loved their neon in this city, he thought, *loved* those bright lights. The pavements were crowded with people and lined with stalls selling everything from rip-off watches to all kinds of junk to hang off your mobile phone. Or scooter key.

He'd been going to tell Palmer that he had Aiko's scooter

and would meet him at the hotel, if he'd tell him how to get there, but now he was glad someone was coming to get him. The thought of another nerve-shredding ride through Tokyo – only this time at night – did not appeal. He'd come back and get the scooter tomorrow.

Adam felt drained and completely tensed at the same time. Relief that it now looked like Charlie was OK, even if he still didn't know where she was, countered by the desperation of not knowing how the hell he was going to find Aiko. He looked at the key in his hand. What would Palmer do if he took off now and went in search of Keiko's apartment? What would his parents say if he didn't call them?

This was tearing him up, so many bloody questions. Was Aiko safe now? Had Yoshi really let her go unharmed? Alice had no reason to lie, Yoshi had no reason to hurt her, but how could he trust a word either of them said? Until he actually saw her, or at least spoke to her, he wouldn't know for sure either way. But one thing was for certain, he wasn't going to find her tonight; he absolutely *had* to go back to the hotel with Palmer, he had to call his parents and take the shit storm that was going to descend on him when he did. That was not going to be pretty.

As he waited for Palmer to turn up – nervous about what was going to happen, agitated he wasn't looking for Aiko – he thought about Alice, not really able to get his head round what she'd done and what she was now doing. How much of what she'd told him was the truth and how much just scrambled shit in her head, he'd no idea. What was totally obvious was that she'd got herself a pretty solid coke habit; could that mean Steve, and possibly even Charlie, had one too? He didn't think so, he was pretty sure he'd guessed the correct scenario and that it was Alice who was entirely responsible for them taking off. She was clearly glued to Yoshi now, and what a lovely couple they made.

He felt bad – not guilty, but somehow responsible – about leaving her there in that room. Walking down the stairs, part of him, the headstrong dragon-slayer, had wanted to go right back up and insist she came with him, but the pragmatist ruled that you couldn't argue with endless lines of coke and an automatic pistol. Plus the other two men he'd seen on the way out. Not if you wanted to celebrate another birthday, down the pub with your mates.

Adam rubbed his cheek, still tender from Yoshi's vicious, diamond-tipped backhander. He couldn't believe how easily the whole situation had got so incredibly out of hand: one stupid phone call, a few flame-fanning lines in a tabloid newspaper and his whole family had gone into a lethal tail-spin, believing that, because it had happened to a girl before, the same awful fate had also befallen Charlie. The worst of all options must have occurred, until proven other-wise. The things human beings did to themselves.

Which brought him right back to Alice.

Could you abandon someone to their fate if they'd chosen it for themselves? She was an adult: what she did or didn't do was up to her, except he wanted to believe that an Alice who wasn't quite so strung out wouldn't have done what she did. Though he realised that was a bit like saying blame the gun not the person who pulls the trigger. This was all about choices. Nobody ever got harangued to take drugs, have a fag or a drink. They were always offered, very nicely. It was always your choice. Alice had made hers, and right now the thought of lighting up a long, pristine white, Virginia king-size was extremely tempting . . .

*   *   *

'So your sister was never kidnapped, then?'

'Doesn't look like it.' Adam, slumped in the passenger seat of a nondescript Toyota hatchback, felt like someone had taken his batteries out.

'And did her friend say where she was?'

'Says she doesn't know.'

'What's she doing hanging round that part of town?'

Adam looked over at Simon Palmer. Either he was naive to the point of being dense or he was fishing for information, and Adam wasn't at all sure how much he should say about Alice, or if he should really be saying anything. He felt an odd sense of loyalty – because he had kind of grown up believing that just talking to authority about your mates was almost the same as grassing them up – even though Alice was hardly a friend any more. He really wanted to download what had happened to him, though, and maybe Palmer, a complete stranger, was actually the right person. Detached, no baggage, what did he care?

'Are you like the law here?'

'In Tokyo?'

'Yeah.'

'No.'

'If I tell you stuff, d'you have to tell the Japanese cops?'

'All depends what it is, Adam.'

Oh, sod it. 'Alice is hanging out with a real GTA villain and –'

'GTA?'

'Grand Theft Auto, the PlayStation game?'

'Yeah, yeah . . . GTA, I'm with you.'

Adam looked at him; he didn't look like a gamer, but it was hard to tell. 'Anyway, she's turned into this total revenge demon and he's like probably a dealer and stuff and he pulled a stinking *gun* on me! Cocked the hammer back and everything . . . pulled the trigger, man. Really.' He opened his window a couple of centimetres. 'She told me she called my parents to get her own back for Charlie stealing her boyfriend, can you believe that? All this because her sodding boyfriend got fed up with her fooling around with some cheap hood. She says she went back to their apartment one day and they'd just gone, but who knows, she could've made the whole thing up, everything . . . except I don't think she knows where they are.'

'Well, they must still be in the country, somewhere.'

'Why?'

'If Charlie had left Japan, her name would have come up when they checked Customs and Immigration records.'

'You think?'

'I know.' Palmer indicated he was turning left as he slowed down and came to a stop at a set of lights. 'And what about your friend, the one they took from that hotel – Aiko?'

'Alice said that they let her go – Yoshi didn't want her, he wanted me.'

'D'you know why?'

'Why me?' Palmer nodded as the lights changed and he accelerated away. 'Yoshi wanted to tell me to bugger off and leave Alice alone.' Palmer glanced at Adam, frowning. 'Honest, that's what she said, I kid you not. She said she freaked when she saw me in Roppongi cos she didn't think anyone'd come looking for Charlie. She just wanted me to go away.'

'And they just let your friend go?'

'That's what she said.'

'While you're calling your parents, I'll get in touch with the police and see if they've heard anything.'

Adam felt as if he'd hit the ground with a jarring thud. Reality check. He'd be talking to his parents in a matter of minutes. And while 'sorry' might have worked on Yoshi, there was *no* way on this earth it was going to be good enough for his mum and dad; he was going to fry.

Sitting on the chair next to the desk in the room he'd been checked into, Adam listened to the familiar English ringing tone, imagining Badger barking as the phone rang in his house. It was something he'd done ever since Badger was a puppy, same when the doorbell went or the post arrived, and no amount of telling had ever made him stop. He was so lost in thinking about Badger that when the phone was answered – some man's voice saying the number – he'd momentarily forgotten who he was calling.

'Uh, anyone there?'

'Dad?'

'Adam? Thank God you're safe! Why did you take so long to call? The man from the embassy said it would be hours ago . . .'

'Right . . .' Palmer had told Adam about the promise he'd made his parents before he knew about the disappearing act; the least Adam could do was help him out. 'I, um, had to stay at the police station longer than they thought, sorry. We just got to the hotel a few minutes ago, been checking in and stuff.'

Silence. Adam imagined this was how a condemned man must feel, waiting for the trap door to open.'

Finally his father cleared his throat. 'Well?'

'Oh, yeah . . . right . . . ah, I'm sorry, OK? For everything.'

'I should bloody well think so, but what I was *waiting* for was any news about Charlie . . . you actually *being* there in Tokyo. You know, if that's all right with you?'

Ah, sarcasm. How he'd missed the old man's favourite weapon in his verbal armoury. 'Yeah, well I haven't *seen* her, but it looks like she was never kidnapped and she's still somewhere here in Japan, travelling round. The man from the embassy, Palmer, he said that's what she's probably doing. She's not phoned or anything, then?'

'No, she hasn't. Neither of you appear to be very good at keeping in touch when you're away. No definite news, then?'

'She hasn't been kidnapped, Dad, really.'

'OK – hang on a sec, your mum wants a word . . .'

Oh, I bet she does – Adam changed ears – and that word would be toxic, he thought, and probably unrepeatable in polite company, knowing his mum.

'You . . .' a deep breath, exhale, 'are in *so* much trouble . . .'

Oh yes, pure venom. 'Look, Mum, I'm –'

'That's all she wants to say, for the moment, Adam.'

'Dad?'

'Yes. Your mother says she wants you here when she does this; wants to see your face.'

'Jeez . . .'

'He will not be of much help, I'm afraid. Now, when I get off the phone from you I'm going to cancel our flights – and you'd better hope I can reclaim some of the money back, or you'll have an even bigger bill – and I want you to get yourself on the next available plane home. OK?'

'Right . . .'

'See you soon, then.'

Adam put the phone down. Still on Death Row. Execution postponed.

32

And I got to know the permanence of all things

Just like at Keiko's apartment, breakfast at the hotel Simon Palmer had booked him into was an alien encounter, and not only that, he'd have to pay extra for it as well. Adam was sure he'd be able to get something more recognisable somewhere between the hotel and where he'd left the scooter the night before, even on a Sunday.

When he'd checked his key in at the front desk the receptionist had handed over an envelope with his name typewritten on it in capital letters. Inside, a note from Simon informed him that he'd be flying back to London the next day on the 9:38 a.m. Virgin flight from Narita and that he had to be at the airport at around 7:30. Which meant catching a train from Ueno Station at 6:15; a ticket for the journey was included. 'Apologies for the early start,' the note ended, 'only flight time available.' Yeah, right. More like getting even for his going AWOL from the police station.

Adam looked at his watch: 10:15. This time tomorrow he'd be thousands of feet up, flying west. Home. He swallowed as he felt his gut tense, stomach muscles bruised and tender . . . he just *had* to find Aiko. He felt bad that he hadn't gone out again the previous night, after talking to his parents, but he'd just slowed to a crawl, eaten something at the hotel's restaurant, gone to his room and crashed, sleeping right through till nine o'clock.

He felt a whole lot better now, and a few minutes spent with the trusty Rough Guide and the crude, over-photocopied map the receptionist had given him and Adam was on his way to the subway – one change and four stops away from Shinjuku, the nearest station to where he'd left the scooter.

There were, he remembered, sixty exits from Shinjuku, and when Adam got off the train he found himself in this huge, bustling, complicated and totally confusing underground city with shops and wide, sprawling boulevards filled with people. What the place must be like during rush hour he could only imagine.

Half an hour later he found Aiko's scooter, helmet still under the seat, exactly where he'd left it. All he had to do now was find his way to Keiko's apartment building. Nothing to it. Adam had all day, with nothing else planned, and he could get as lost as he liked. He looked across the road, down the side street leading into the cramped network of sleaze where he'd found Alice; hard to admit it, but there was no point in even thinking about her now.

Physically turning his back on Kabukicho, he pushed Alice out of his head and focused on the immediate problem – that he only had the roughest idea of how to get to where he was supposed to be going, and had only been there once before, in the dark; plus the fact that the scooter was getting low on fuel and one thing he hadn't seen since he'd been in Tokyo was a petrol station. Not one. Not that they'd been top of his list of sights to look out for.

Just how much mileage he had left in the tank was a mystery, but when he'd switched on the ignition, the indicator needle hovered uncomfortably close to empty. If he ran out . . . he'd work out what he'd do if he ran out when and if it happened. Clamping the helmet back on his head he pulled on the rear brake lever, pressed the electric start, revved the engine as it turned over and set off. Doing what was probably an illegal U-ey at the next set of lights, Adam went back down the road to the next intersection and turned right.

One street of bland apartment blocks looked pretty much like the next, and the fact that there were convenience stores on a lot of them didn't help much either, as he couldn't remember if he and Aiko had been into an am:pm, a Lawson's or a Family Mart to buy the flowers for Keiko. Things finally began to fall into place when he rode past the Doutor coffee shop he was positive was the one they'd gone to for breakfast.

He stopped, went back and pulled up outside it, mentally retracing the route they'd taken to get there. Then he checked the traffic and accelerated off to see if he was right. Turning left at the end of the street, and then almost immediately right, he spotted the tree by which they'd parked the scooter and opposite it saw a Lawson 24-hour convenience store; through the window he could see bunches of flowers like the one they'd bought. Adam parked up in the same place, and was prising off the helmet when it occurred to him that he didn't know Keiko's apartment number. Terrific.

Adam looked up at the building, racking his brains. It was either on the ninth or tenth floor; he thought probably the

tenth for some reason. And it was on the right of the stairwell as he looked at the building, further away from the
tree, rather than near to it . . . he remembered turning left
out of the lift, could picture the street as he'd seen it when
he'd looked out of the window. Small clues, but they were
all he had and they'd have to do.

Walking up to the entrance he went over to the panel of
numbered entryphone buttons, a row of four for each of the
twelve floors, going from 0101 up to 1204. If he had to
make a stab at it, Keiko's apartment was either 0903 or
more likely 1003. He pressed the button for 1003. No reply.
He pressed it again, for slightly longer, but no one
answered. OK, he could've been wrong . . . better try Option
2. He pressed 0903 and a couple of seconds later he heard
a man's voice.

'*Hai?*'

'Hello . . . is Keiko there? Kei-ko?'

'*Nan des ka?*'

'KEIKO.'

'*Dare?*'

'Sorry . . . I, um, I think I've got the wrong apartment.'

'*Nan no yoji desuka?*'

Adam shrugged, pressed 1003 again, just in case, and
then stood back near the road to look up at the tenth floor.
What the hell was he going to do now? He'd kind of
assumed Keiko would be home – she *should* be home! This
was maximum frustration, to have found the right place, be
standing in front of the actual building and for Keiko not to
be there.

Did he sit outside until she came back, like some lost
puppy? It was a plan, but not one he fancied putting into
action very much; this was his last day, and to spend it here

would be just so depressing. Keiko could be out all day – for all he knew the shop where she worked was open – and on the other hand, she might come home at any moment. Dilemma, dilemma, dilemma.

His stomach growled, demanding an answer. He hadn't actually stopped anywhere for breakfast after leaving the hotel and he had a substantial space to fill. A good compromise would be to go to the coffee shop, have something to eat and then come back and see if anything had changed.

An hour later nothing had. Still no one home. Adam bought a cheap biro from the store, took a napkin as he left and wrote a short note, in capitals, which spelled out the hotel where he was staying, its telephone number and his name. God, he hoped Keiko was going to understand the message when she got it. Locking the helmet under the seat, he wrapped the key in the napkin and posted it in apartment 1003's post box. He was done. All over now bar the flying home.

Walking away he felt completely deflated. An undeniable sense of failure descended on him, clinging like wet clothes, almost impossible to shake off. Nothing had worked out, really, except that it didn't look like Charlie was in any kind of trouble. A result of some sort, he supposed. And he'd found Alice – though, as it turned out, she didn't want to be – but he'd lost Aiko and couldn't see how he'd ever find her again. God, how depressing was *that* thought? And of course he was to blame for all the crap that was going to be dumped on him from a great height.

A week ago – only seven stupid days – he'd been so damn sure of everything, so positive he was doing the right thing. So self-righteous about the fact that it was him actually doing *something* while everyone else sat in a virtual coma doing sweet FA. And what had he achieved? Apart from spending a lot of his dad's money, and a fair chunk of his own, he had to remind himself, not a huge amount. He'd go back home, get his ear chewed off, be grounded for ever, and be broke till God knew when paying his dad back. He'd still be at college, still be with Suzy . . . what the hell was he going to do about Suzy?

Adam stopped. This was SO depressing! He had got to stop doing this shit to himself. Really. Maybe he should just go to a bar and get rat-arsed. With a 5:00 am start the next day? OK, maybe not rat-arsed, just bladdered. He could go back to the Gaspanic, you never knew, maybe Kenichi and Ayumi would be there. With Aiko. And then again, maybe not, but anything would be better than mooching around, mentally digging a hole for himself to sit in and metaphorically slit his wrists. He checked the map and found the nearest subway station was Meiji-jingúmae.

Coming out of a side road Adam found himself in a crowded nightmare of a street that looked a lot like Camden, except the road was so narrow and jammed with so many people that you could hardly move, every centimetre of space packed with posters, cheap jewellery, expensive retro clothes, food, *'I went to Tokyo and all I got was this lousy T-shirt'* type of shops, girls yelling at the crowds through small plastic megaphones, boys standing holding up signs saying that, whatever it was, you could find it at Thank You Mart for only ¥390. It was extreme shopping for the under-25s. Retail mayhem.

As Adam wove his way through the mass of bodies it made him think this was what it would be like for a blood corpuscle as it was pumped through a vein or an artery. When he reached the end of the street and found himself on a main thoroughfare, flanked on the side opposite him by a massive wall of trees, he realised that he hadn't been pushed or shoved once by anyone. Like they all had personal radar, allowing them to avoid bodily contact. He looked back the way he'd come and wouldn't have believed it possible if he hadn't just done it.

Making his way down towards the subway station, he began to notice something odd. There were a lot of really weirdly dressed people, all going his way; all, now he looked more closely, girls. It was like everyone was on their way to a really incredibly serious fancy dress party, and for all Adam knew, they were.

In front of him was a girl with her hair sculpted so that she looked like some 3D version of Sonic the Hedgehog; her friend, dressed all in black, was wearing incredibly high-heeled black vinyl ankle boots and a black vinyl pillbox hat. Both had dead white face make-up and matt-black lipstick. Looking back Adam saw other similarly dressed girls, and up ahead, at a set of lights, costumed figures were streaming across the road to join even more of them.

There were platinum-blonde girls in bondage kimonos wearing wings made out of real feathers; there were girls who looked like a cross between a Victorian housemaid and a road accident victim; and groups all dressed identically, like cult members who'd been recently let out of an Institute for the Unhinged Fashion Victim. There were stylish, absolutely beautiful girls, scarily ugly mutant punks and the simply bizarre, genderless look that defied description.

What the hell was going on?

Did he care?

Not really. Frankly my dear, as his dad was so fond of saying, he couldn't give a damn. Adam carried on walking up the road towards the subway.

33

True love why is it shine small like that star?

There had been no one he recognised at the Gaspanic. No Kenichi, no Ayumi and definitely no Aiko. He'd looked, everywhere, but the early afternoon crowd had hidden no surprises. So Adam had left; why stay? Out on the pavement something had drawn him down the street to the Hobgoblin British pub and a seat at its long wooden bar.

Where he'd had a couple of beers.

And a couple or three more.

He'd talked to an American software designer sitting next to him at the bar, but mostly he'd nursed his beers, thinking about going to the vending machine and buying a packet of fags, staring at a football game on the widescreen plasma TV, remembering everything he could about the last kiss, trying to recall exactly how Aiko had looked as her face came up to his, her eyelids fluttering like the wings of small creatures. Torturing himself with the fact that it now looked like it really had been the last time he would ever be with her.

If he couldn't figure out a way of getting in touch with Aiko, how the hell was she ever going to find him? Always assuming, after what she'd been through, that she wanted to. Would she have gone to the police after Yoshi let her go, or just gone home and tried to forget it'd ever happened? His only hope was that Keiko would understand his note and pass the information on to Aiko. And if she did, sitting in a pub getting pissed was not going to help.

Adam sat up; he should be back at the hotel in case she phoned, was what he *should* be doing. He looked round and saw that his American pal had gone without saying goodbye, which said a lot about the quality of his conversation. The man's empty Guinness glass and a screwed-up paper coaster were still on the bar. Along with a book of matches and a soft pack of unfiltered Lucky Strikes. The real Yankee deal, like his dad had smoked, when he'd smoked, not the 'made under licence' excuses for American fags you got sold in England. He picked up the packet and shook it. Empty. Then one last cigarette rattled into sight. He opened the book of matches. One left.

It was a sign. No doubt about it. The condemned man's last cigarette.

Adam shook out the Lucky, broke off the match and struck it, the sharp smell of sulphur stinging his nostrils. He looked at the cigarette. What the hell, it was only the one. He wasn't going to buy any more. He held the match up to the tobacco and inhaled, the smoke hitting his lungs like a slow punch, making him feel light-headed and numbing his fingertips. He exhaled through his nose, tapping ash into the nearby ashtray and taking a second, deeper pull. Oh yes.

A picture flashed in his mind's eye. Alice. Alice and her gold-toothed, diamond geezer dealer. He looked down at the Lucky, smoke curling artistically up from its grey-red tip. Pot. Kettle. Black.

He stubbed out the cigarette, drained his bottle and left the pub.

Back at the hotel there was one message waiting for him. A Suzy Barrett had called. Oh, God, reality really was knocking on his door, demanding to be let back in, but there was no way he could face a long-distance phone conversation with Suzy at the moment. No way. Adam screwed up the note and dropped it in the rubbish-bin-with-sandpit-ashtray by the lifts and went up to his room.

He put the TV on for company and took a long shower to wash the day off, get rid of the smoke'n'beer aroma he'd picked up at the Hobgoblin and de-stress. He thought he might get changed, after drying off, and go out for one last sushi or noodles or whatever, but he felt completely knackered when he came out of the bathroom. Instead, wrapped in the kimono-style dressing gown he'd found on the bed when he came in, Adam lay, propped up on a couple of pillows and channel-hopped until he found the only thing worth watching: a baseball game.

He had no idea when he fell asleep, but when he woke up he was cold, still lying on top of the covers; the game was long over and had been replaced by some kind of Japanese Parkinson-style chat show. Not bothering to check the time he climbed out of the kimono, put on a T-shirt, turned off the TV and the lights and climbed back into the bed. He was fast asleep again in seconds.

Adam knew he'd had this dream before, quite recently. A phone was ringing and he had this very strong feeling it meant something important, but couldn't for the life of him think what it was. And then the sleep wall cracked open

243

and he heard the ringing for real.

But he didn't have a phone in his room.

Shit! Not in *his* room . . . he sat up, groped for the bed-side light, gave up and stumbled over to the desk in the pitch-black, patting the darkness to find where the phone was. Picking up the handset he discovered no one was there. Adam stood in the red glow from the digital display on the front of the TV, looking at the silent phone and then at the display. For some reason it said 05:10; then it said 05:11. And finally everything made sense; that had been an alarm call and he had just over an hour to get to Ueno Station.

He put down the phone and turned on the lights. Funny though, because he'd never ordered an alarm call. Adam could almost hear his brain creak into gear as he worked out that this must mean it was Simon Palmer who'd booked it. He must really want to see the back of him.

With almost no packing to do, he was downstairs at the reception fifteen minutes later and handing over his key. Stopping for a moment, he did one more final check on passport, airline ticket, train ticket and his Passnet card before bowing a thank you to the receptionist and walking out of the hotel and into very early-morning Tokyo. It was a cool, cloudy day and he now had forty-five minutes to get to Ueno and catch the train to Narita. And four hours left in Japan.

Standing in one of those interminable mono-queues, the kind that were apparently supposed to be the fastest way to move people, Adam wondered if there was ever a time when these monster airports weren't busy. Like it was 7:30 in the morning and the place was already packed out and buzzing. He shuffled forward, in that chaingang way these queues made you do, eventually came to the end and then found himself handing his passport and e-ticket to a blonde, English, permatanned woman in a Virgin Atlantic uniform. It was a shock not seeing someone with pale skin, oriental features and straight, black hair.

By just after eight o'clock he had an aisle seat, a baggage check, his passport and a ticket stub. He turned to go through to Duty Free and found himself looking at Aiko, standing twenty metres away, just beyond the final check-in desk.

This, he thought, is when the alarm call *really* happens and I wake up.

But it didn't. Behind him he heard someone ask if he might move so they could get to the desk he was still standing next to, and he realised he was holding his breath.

'Sorry . . .' Adam looked over his shoulder and pasted a smile on for the middle-aged woman behind him. She didn't smile back.

For a moment he felt like he'd forgotten how to walk, then, stuffing his passport and other papers into his small backpack, he broke into a run, still not quite sure this wasn't the most astonishingly realistic dream he'd ever had in his entire life. Any moment now, he was almost sure, the person who looked exactly like Aiko would turn out to be someone else entirely.

'Hello, Adam.'

It was her. Adam came to a halt half a metre in front of Aiko, reached out and touched this person he couldn't possibly ever see again. 'How did you –?'

'Keiko tex me, very like two o'clock, about message. I couldn't sleep, I was awake and call her . . . but I think too late to ring hotel. I ring at six today, but they say you go already to Ueno. So I come. You OK?'

'Me? Yeah . . . yeah, but it's you, what about you? What the hell happened? I mean, I thought you probably wouldn't want to talk to me again after, you know, getting kidnapped by some scuzzy *yakuza*.'

'You want coffee maybe?'

'OK.' Adam looked at his watch: just under an hour until they called the flight. 'Coffee's good – you want a miso soup maybe?'

Aiko smiled. 'Had some.'

Adam took her hand; holding it felt like the missing piece of the jigsaw had just slotted back into place. He looked around for a coffee shop and saw one over to their right. 'How d'you get here, anyway? How'd you know where I was checking in?'

'Got cab, and not too many plane go to London right now. Also, you not so hard to see.'

They found a table and sat down, still holding hands. Getting a coffee would mean letting go and he had so little time. 'Tell me what happened, Aiko . . . what did Yoshi do to you? Alice said he just let you go.'

'You saw Alice?'

Adam nodded. 'I lucked out, found her in Kabukicho, that office where I s'pose they took you? She's so messed up . . .'

'You feel bad?'

'Yeah. She wasn't always like that . . . it was like talking to her evil twin.'

'Not your fault.' Aiko reached over, ran her finger across his lips and then stroked his cheek. 'What happened to you here?'

Adam shrugged. 'Not a lot . . . Yoshi's way of saying goodbye.'

'That Yoshi no good, but Alice must like it to stay.'

'Oh, I think she likes it OK. He didn't hurt you, did he?'

'No. Hit two men who bring me, like a mad man . . . he want you, not me. Jus' told me "get out!".'

'What did you do?'

'Go to Keiko shop.'

'I didn't think I was ever going to see you again. No way of getting in touch, nothing — I don't even know your *surname*, Aiko.'

'Takashi.'

'What?'

'Family name, Takashi. What yours?'

'Mine? Grey, like the colour.' Adam nodded, pointing his thumb at a man walking by. 'Like that bloke's suit.'

'We say *hai-iro*.'

'Right.' Adam looked across at the nearest Departures board, checking his flight number. Still 'Wait in Lounge'.

'You have to go?'

'Uh, no . . . not yet.'

'You find Charlie, Adam . . . Alice say where she is?'

Adam shook his head and looked away. 'No . . . I didn't find her, I don't know where she is or anything.'

'You speak to parents?'

'Oh yes.'

'Not happy?'

'Very not happy.'

'You sorry you came?'

Adam felt Aiko's grip on his hand get tighter and he looked up, completely focused on her, forgetting about tomorrow. 'No.'

'Good.'

'Yeah, very good . . . would've been a lot better if I was

going back with my sister, but nothing's perfect I suppose, right?'

'Nothing perfect, no . . .' Aiko let go of Adam's hand and, as she started delving in her small backpack, he glanced at the Departures board again.

'Shit – gotta make a move, Aiko, my gate's up.' He looked at his watch: 8:50. Where had the time gone?

Aiko pushed a spiral-bound pad and a sparkly pink biro, complete with a tiny furry toy attached to it by a chain, across the table at him. Something was written in the top page. 'My email – you take it, write yours quick.'

'Right, right . . .' Adam tore off the sheet and stuffed it in his back pocket; grabbing the pen he scribbled his email address on the pad, not quite able to compute the reality that it was suddenly time to say goodbye and they hadn't really *said* anything, just kind of chatted, like they had all the time in the world. And now there was none.

They stood up, Adam taking both of Aiko's hands and not knowing what to do next. Lost for words, aware that he was starring in his own soppy, rom-com airport goodbye scene and wondering what Hugh Grant would do in his place.

'Adam, *aishi-té ruwa*.' In a sort of déjà vu-plus of the last 'last kiss', Aiko reached up, pulled Adam to her and proceeded to press every button he owned. Then she stopped. 'You better go.'

'Yeah . . . right . . .' So pretty, yet so practical. She was some combination, this girl. Completely on auto-pilot, Adam picked up his backpack and didn't move. 'Gonna, you know, really miss you.' This was the absolute pits . . . so much to say and all the verbal skills of a dim-witted baboon to do it with . . .

'I know, but you must.' Aiko took his hand and walked

him quickly across to the passport control. As he handed over his passport and ticket, she stood on tip-toe and whispered in his ear. '*Aishi-te ruwa . . .*'

Adam looked at her as he was handed his papers. 'What does that mean?'

Aiko smiled and took a small parcel out of her backpack, giving it to him. 'You find out.'

34

Store my ducks

'What time does the flight come in tomorrow?'

Sitting at the kitchen table, having one last go at the crossword, Tony Grey looked up from his paper. 'Two o'clock. We don't have to be there really until half past, quarter to three; takes at least that long to get your luggage and go through customs. Are we both going to go?'

'Don't you think so? United front, say what we both have to say once and not have to repeat ourselves? Seems like the best way to handle it. At least this way one of us can concentrate on the driving while the other one loses it with him in the back.'

'He's going to wish he'd stayed in Tokyo.'

'Don't get me started. I want to save my anger for tomorrow.' Sarah Grey looked at the oven clock. 'It's almost one o'clock, I'm going up; you coming?'

'Yeah . . . 24 across, "made to eat", five and three, F three blanks E, blank E blank. Any ideas? All I can think of is "ready meal", and that wouldn't fit if you crowbarred it in.'

Sarah stopped as she was going out into the hall. 'Force fed.'

'Ah . . . right . . . thanks.' Tony wrote the answer in.

'D'you think if we put a notice outside saying "no junk

mail" anyone'd take any notice?'

'Sorry?'

'Yet more take-away flyers.' Sarah shook her head. 'I swear they make up a quarter of what we recycle.'

Tony went into rote mode, checking the back door, unplugging the kettle and the portable TV and finally turning off the kitchen lights. When he walked in to the hall he found Sarah standing by the front door, holding something in her hands, tears streaming down her cheeks.

'What's the matter? What is it?'

Sarah held out the single piece of card and Tony took it, seeing a picture – trees, the sea – on one side and writing on the other. He looked at Sarah.

'There was a Post-it note on it.' She was holding a square of yellow paper. 'Stupid postman delivered it to the wrong bloody house number . . . they've been meaning to drop it in for days, the note says.'

Tony focused back on the card. '"*Have been doing the islands, as far away from the cities as we can get. Been to Oki-shoto and Sado gashima – so beautiful! – and are now up north near Russia on the Noto peninsula.*"

'She's OK . . .'

Life. Hearts. Birth. Seed. Spirits. Wish. Real.

The walk from the passport control to the baggage X-ray, clutching the parcel, trying to keep Aiko in view for as long as possible, had been like a waking dream. Unreal. The saddest thing. Interminable. It was if he was being pulled by an invisible, irresistible force which took his bag and his coat and the parcel and fed them into the X-ray machine and out the other side.

When Adam joined his belongings, having been processed by the metal detector, Aiko had gone and he was alone, surrounded by milling crowds, in bright, shiny, buy-me-now Duty Freeland.

The whole of his journey to the gate was a blur; he felt completely detached from what he was doing, still operating on automatic while he tried to make sense of what he'd been through over the last five days. As an exercise in not thinking about Aiko it wasn't a huge success.

From the crowded room where everyone was sitting round waiting to get on the plane, they were all eventually herded out through the tunnel and then there he was, in his aisle seat, seat belt on and checking out what movies there were to watch over the next twelve hours.

This was it, then. Next stop Heathrow. Mental parentals, college, Suzy, the whole rest of his sorry life. All the crap to deal with, all at once; it couldn't really get much worse. And out there, somewhere, Charlie. Who had *no* idea what had been going on, the trouble she'd caused since she took off with her ex-best friend's boyfriend. One email, one little bloody postcard, and none of this would've happened, *everything* would be different. Except Alice. Alice would still be a screw-up.

By the time the crew were readying for take-off and the safety vid was running on the seat back screen, Adam still didn't have anyone sitting next to him. Result! Reaching down to get his backpack and have it by him he saw Aiko's parcel, which he'd forgotten he'd put on the floor as well.

He picked it up. Wrapped in paper covered in cartoon rabbits, it was the size and flexibility of a small paperback. He carefully picked at a corner of clear sticky tape, pulled it down slowly so as not to tear the wrapping and opened the parcel.

A Japanese/English phrasebook.

Adam cracked a grin; very funny. He was trying to remember exactly what it was that Aiko had whispered to him – ashi-tey something? – so he could look it up, when he saw there was a piece of paper tucked into the book. Pulling it out, he unfolded it once and then a second time, expecting a letter but instead seeing a page from a calendar. August.

There was a beautiful photograph of a white-faced geisha, her sculpted hair decorated with silver ornaments and yellow flowers, and underneath it the month written in half a dozen languages. Then he noticed that the 26th was circled in biro

and had something written by it in tiny capitals. He turned on
his overhead light and read:

HERE I COME TO LONDON, TO STUDY!

THE END/OWARI

Acknowledgements

Acknowledgements

I would like to thank a few people, without whom this story would have been a lot harder to tell. In Tokyo I had help and assistance from Rei Uemura, Olly Denton, Robin Probyn, David Peace and William Miller; special thanks must go to Laura and Giichi Inoue for unique insights and great hospitality, with a very special mention for Kenichi Yoshioka, who rescued a stranded visitor. Once again, Sarah Odedina and Georgia Murray have been the sharpest and most enthusiastic editors, and many thanks to Yuriko Kishida for making sure I didn't get lost in translation.